Impact

Book 1

Authentic Stories of the Transgender Community Series

Helen Dale

ISBN 978-1-7397667-1-9

Acknowledgements

I am grateful to members of Manchester Women's Writers' group for their critiques of many of the chapters and to Jo Whalley and Sally McKenzie who edited the manuscript for me.

The cover illustration incorporates sections of photographs from Unsplash contributors Yang Dawei and Charlie Deets.

Language

Impact is set in 1997-8 and uses language and terminology in common use at that time.

Impact

Book 1.   1997

Chapter 1.   Impact
Tuesday 11th March 1997

Oh shit! I knew, as soon as I glanced in my mirror, that the car behind hadn't a hope of stopping before it hit me as I came to rest behind other vehicles in the outside lane of the M1. I pulled on the hand brake. Shit! Shit! Shit! Why today, of all days? I braced myself for the impact.

The collision itself wasn't that bad – but the consequences were likely to be huge.

Bugger! Shit! FUCK! I rested my head on the steering wheel and just sat there.

The driver of the car that had hit me rapped on the window. I rolled it down. "Are you OK, love?" he asked. I just nodded my head then got out of my Cavalier SRi, straightening my skirt as I stood up, and went to the back of the car to check out the damage. There was a slight dent in the bodywork – otherwise nothing. Even the lights were all undamaged. I might get away with it after all.

"Doesn't look serious, obviously my insurance company will take care of it," the other driver assured me. "Here's my card – and I've written the insurance details on the back. Can I have your details?"

I got out a piece of paper and wrote C L Williamson and my address and insurance company details and handed it to him.

By now, the police had arrived and were checking if there were any injuries and helping us to get our vehicles onto the hard shoulder. When I gave the officer my licence his eyebrows raised as he looked at my face then back at the licence.

"Is there a problem?" I asked.

"I guess not." He replied. "We need to carry out breathalyser checks on everyone involved though so can you come to our car?"

That would be the least of my problems as I hadn't had a drink in days.

As I got in the patrol car, the officer who had checked my licence showed his colleague his notebook – he then glanced at me and a smirk appeared on his face.

I sighed. Ignorant pigs.

The test completed, the officer confirmed it was negative and, as I'd been the victim rather than the cause of the crash, my car was still roadworthy and we'd exchanged insurance details, I was free to go on my way.

I lit a cigarette and inhaled the smoke deeply before pulling back onto the main carriageway and heading south. If the insurance company did get involved, my wife's and my initials are the same. I'm Christopher Lionel – useful as 'Chris' fits both male and female, she's Carol Lucinda but prefers her middle name as it sounds posher – though she wouldn't put it in those terms. So, if the other driver reported having hit a woman's car, the details would still tally. With luck, there would be no further contact – especially if I didn't bother to make a claim. I might be able to straighten the dent myself; a bit of body-filler a quick spray job and it wouldn't be noticeable.

A few miles further on, I pulled off the motorway and drove across country then turned onto a back road that ran alongside an old gravel pit now filled with water and found a concealed and totally unoccupied area just off the road I knew of. I parked the car so the open door would provide some cover from anyone else pulling into the area as well as giving me the chance to drive off quickly if I needed to. It was just getting dark and I grabbed my bag of clothes from the boot. I sat back down with my legs out of the car, removed my tights and knickers from underneath my skirt and pulled on my pants, trousers and socks. On, too, with slip-on shoes – then a padded jacket. I closed the door again and removed my wig then proceeded to remove my make-up. OK – now if anyone saw me there was nothing untoward to attract attention.

Now for the final stage, which always made me nervous as I was most exposed – open the jacket and undo the buttons of my blouse – then off with the jacket, blouse and bra before pulling on a shirt. Well, that had been the plan when a police Panda car pulled in next to me. For crying out loud, this really wasn't my bloody day. As the officer got out of his car, I zipped up my jacket again.

I rolled down the window as he approached.

"Good evening, sir. Can I ask what you're doing here?"

"Nothing. Just taking a break on my way home."

"I see. You seem a bit nervous, sir."

He was looking at my holdall on the seat next to me, unzipped.

"Can I ask what you've got in the holdall?"

"Just clothes. Why?"

"Unusual to have the bag on the passenger seat. Most people would put it in the boot or on the back seat. May I have a look in it?"

Sweat formed on my forehead. I didn't think he had any right to insist on looking in the bag – but if I refused, it would certainly make him even more suspicious. I reached over and pulled the bag onto my lap and opened the top. He shone his torch into the bag. As I knew they would be, the wig, panties, tights and shoes I'd removed were on top of my shirt.

"Yours, *sir*?" he asked.

"Yes," I admitted. "It's not illegal, is it?"

"No, sir," he replied with emphasis on the 'sir'.

"So, what are you doing here?" he asked again.

"I'm getting changed. Why?"

"Well. sir." Again, that sarcastic pause. "It's just that there's a sailing club across the road and there have been thefts of equipment from some of the boats so we've been asked to keep an eye on the place. Now, if what you've told me is true, then there's nothing to worry about. But, if there are any problems reported tonight, I've got your vehicle number and we'll know where to find you. Goodnight."

With that, he returned to his car and drove off.

I finished changing, repacked my bag and put it into the boot. I lit another cigarette and stood outside the car while I smoked it trying to avoid getting the smell of the smoke on my male clothes. It wasn't just the crossdressing the family didn't know of. When I got back into the car, I ate an orange then wiped the peel around my face to, hopefully, disguise any lingering smell of smoke or make-up.

As I drove the last few miles home, I was relieved the police hadn't taken any more interest in me than they had. Cross-dressing wasn't illegal, but all too often police would find some reason to be difficult or would be downright offensive – and could maliciously "out" you.

And *that* could easily cost you your job – not to mention your marriage and family. I dreaded to think how Lucinda, my wife, would react to discovering my secret. She seemed to be becoming increasingly prejudiced since joining a 'happy-clappy' church with links to homophobic evangelical movements in America.

So why did we do it?

The simple answer is because we have to. There is a side to us that can only be satisfied by cross-dressing. Believe me, we TRY to stop. Ask almost any tranny and they'll tell you about the times they've purged – getting rid of their collection of clothes, wigs and make-up. Then something, often insignificant, would start you off again.

Chapter 2.   It's Tuesday so it's Shepherds' Pie
Tuesday 11th March 1997

I pulled the car onto the drive and opened the left-hand garage door. Having driven the car inside, I had another look at the dent. I was sure it could be fixed easily; the car was twelve years old and there were a couple of other scratches so it wouldn't affect the value. Not that I had any plans to sell it in any case.

I closed the up-and-over door, locked it, then walked round to the front door – noting that the grass would definitely need mowing at the weekend. We hadn't needed a four-bedroom house – but Lucinda had wanted to move to the village to be near a friend and it meant that we had a master bedroom, our daughter Olivia had her own bedroom and a playroom / study/ menagerie which doubled as a guest room – leaving an office for me. As soon as the front door was opened, I was attacked by our two Pugs.

"Is that you Chris?" called Lucinda.

"Yes, love," I replied – who else did she think would be using a key in the front door?

"Shepherds' pie for dinner, is that OK?"

"Fine with me." Well, come on. It's Tuesday so of course it was shepherds' pie, just as tomorrow would be lamb chops and Thursday would be fish fingers. Not that I'm criticising – it was just the well-established routine that we'd developed to fit in with both of us working. And we did both need to work with the mortgage we had on the house, a mortgage that had jumped by 2% in the month between signing contracts and completion.

Having given Lucinda a quick kiss, I told her I was going for a shower – even with the orange peel trick, I wanted to ensure that any last traces of perfume and cigarette smoke really had been eliminated. She warned me not to be too long as dinner was nearly ready.

As we ate, we discussed our days.

Olivia told us that she'd been selected for the hockey team – playing on the right wing while her best friend, June, would be in goal. The next match was an away game in Bedford so she would need picking up after the match.

I told them about the shunt on the motorway and assured a very worried Olivia that I was completely unhurt and that the damage was slight. I also told Lucinda that Ed, my line manager, wanted to see me in the office the next day. The company was doing fine – sales were going through the roof and he seemed more than happy with my work so it was unlikely to be trouble. It might even be a promotion and a pay rise.

Dinner over, Olivia asked if I could help her with her maths homework so we left her mum to do the dishes while we went up to her study. Homework over and dishes done and put away, we all gathered in the lounge for the evening's television. The two dogs took their usual places; Max in front of the fire, Maya sitting on Olivia's lap.

Chapter 3.   Two Coffees
Wednesday 12th March 1997

The next morning, I drove down to our offices in Borehamwood. Having parked, I walked through the main entrance and after getting a smile from Linda on reception, ran up the stairs. I took pride in the fact I was fitter than most of my colleagues. After dropping my briefcase at my desk, I stuck my head round Ed's door.

"Come in Chris, coffee?"

"Morning Ed, yes please"

Denise didn't need to ask how we took them. She'd been Ed's secretary before I joined the department and that was more than 3 years ago.

With the coffees in front of us, Ed got down to the point.

"You know the organisation is building a new distribution centre near Manchester to service the midlands and northwest?"

"Yes, it was announced at the conference, wasn't it?" I confirmed.

"What hasn't been publicised is it will be more than just a northern distribution centre. Property costs in the southeast are horrendous and trying to get decent staff is difficult – so they want to move any departments up there that don't need to be near London. We're going to set up a new IT centre for the whole organisation. I want you to manage the project. Are you interested? You'll have to spend at least 2-3 days per week in Manchester; possibly more at times as work gets underway – but it will mean promotion and another five thousand a year. Because of the travel involved, you'll also get a company car – and an allowance for being away from home so much."

Five thousand – that's a 25 per cent pay rise. Plus a car. That would make a heck of a difference to our finances. And in Manchester – that would be great!

"I'm certainly interested – but I'll have to talk it over with Lucinda and Olivia. I can't really see them raising any problems though. What car band are we talking about by the way?" I asked.

"Probably band 3 – so Vectra, BMW 3 series or equivalent. The project will start seriously in a couple of months – but there'll be trips up there before then."

"Sounds good to me – I'll talk it over with the family this evening. How much work has been planned already, what's the timescale and milestones and what's the budget for the work?"

We spent a couple of hours going over the specifications that had been drafted and the rough scope of the project. We tossed some ideas around as though I'd already confirmed my acceptance – well, realistically, that was a forgone conclusion.

Chapter 4.   Lamb Chops
Wednesday 12th March 1997

nitially, I'll probably spend one or two nights a week away – which isn't that different to now. It will build up, though and probably mean driving up there on a Monday and coming back on Friday eventually. There may even be times when I need to be away for the weekend at times." I explained as Lucinda served the lamb chops.

"We won't have to move there, will we? All our friends are around here. And I don't want Olivia having to change schools," Lucinda said as she spooned mashed potato onto our plates to join the lamb chops and cauliflower. "Bring the mint sauce and gravy to the table please, Olivia."

"No, we won't have to move up there permanently unless they moved the whole company and, even then I'd just look for another job down here," I assured her as we took our seats.

"Will you be here for my birthday? Who will help me with my homework?" Olivia had her priorities sorted.

"I'm sure I can arrange to be here for your birthday and we'll still be able to talk on the phone, love," I assured her. "And it's probably at least six months before I'm away for more than two or three nights a week."

"We can certainly do with the extra money – and you having a company car means I can use ours all the time I suppose." Lucinda had her own priorities. "Maybe we can get those curtains I wanted from Debenhams," she added – confirming my suspicions she had already planned how some of that extra money would be spent.

I had my own reasons for wanting to take on the project and the extra money was not the most important. Manchester had one of the most tranny friendly scenes in the country. I'd enjoyed a few good evenings out in the Gay Village and this project could mean a lot more.

Chapter 5.   Just a Coke, I'm driving
Wednesday 2nd April 1997

Three weeks later, I drove past the scene of the shunt that had nearly caused me to have a heart attack. This time I was heading north in my brand-new BMW 318 company car. It had that fabulous new car smell, so I had to be careful to keep the windows open when I smoked. I'd chosen the midnight blue version with cream interior and alloy wheels. It looked great but there was nothing to make it stand out – I didn't want anyone recognising my car when driving dressed en-femme. It was a Tuesday afternoon and I'd be stopping in Manchester for two nights while holding meetings. The boot contained my usual suitcase that Lucinda had seen me pack – plus the sports bag she knew nothing about.

The M6 around the top of Birmingham was the usual drag. It really had to be the most depressing stretch of motorway I knew. I wished that the proposed northern relief road was already opened. Then it was on past Stafford and Stoke and onto the final stretch before Knutsford where I'd leave the M6 to cut over to the M56. Why on earth hadn't the planners included a link directly from the M6 to the M56? Madness!

The hotel near the airport was ideal for my purposes. It was an acceptable price for the company and convenient for the project office we'd set up nearby. Most important, as far as I was concerned, it had a side entrance that did not go past reception – ideal for me to come and go without being observed. And it was only a fifteen-minute drive to Canal Street.

Wednesday, I had end-to-end meetings from nine in the morning until four in the afternoon including a visit to the proposed site for the new premises. Once these were finished, I could head for my room on the 6th floor, pour myself a small glass of wine and relax, watching the aircraft flying in and out of the nearby airport while my bath filled. Then a long soak in gloriously scented bubbles. Heaven.

Next, it was time to dress to kill. We I, my version anyway. I'd always adopted more of a "woman-next-door" look than six-inch stilettos or thigh-high boots – and miniskirts that were little more than deep belts in which some of the girls strutted their stuff. Not that I had anything against those who favoured that look – but it just wasn't me. I put on my undies then sat in front of the mirror to do my face. I'd already shaved using a new double-bladed wet razor to get as close as possible. Then it was a green stick to hide any remaining redness from the facial hair – followed by Max Factor stick foundation. If I'd been staying dressed more than 4 or 5 hours, I'd use Dermablend as a base but for just an evening, Max Factor was adequate, a lot less expensive and had a more natural finish. Blusher, eyeliner, mascara and eye shadow followed, then lipstick to complete the picture. I savoured every step. Nearly time for the wig – I'd often thought of saving up for a real hair wig – but they need so much care and, like most transvestites, I had to store my kit in a sports bag which isn't conducive to good wig care. Instead, mine was one from a specialist supplier in London – with mixed shades of light brown giving a natural appearance. I'd also had it trimmed to suit my face.

Before the wig, though, I finished dressing in a red caftan-style top over a black knee-length skirt from C&A. Finally, I slipped on my black court shoes with two-inch heels. My nightdress was laid out on the pillow ready for later – I certainly wouldn't be wearing pyjamas while away from home.

Checking my handbag, I ensured that I had cash with me, compact and lipstick for repairs later in the evening, car keys and room key. I really didn't want to have to go to reception and tell them I'd locked myself out of my room. Though I did have a spare bag of male clothes in the boot just in case.

Then it was down in the lift to the first floor, along the corridor, down a flight of stairs to the back door – my car was parked in one of the spaces nearby.

I always got a thrill slipping behind the wheel when dressed. It wasn't sexual. It just felt "right" somehow.

Out onto Princess Parkway and into town. Through Moss Side – making sure my doors were locked – then up onto the Mancunian Way for a few hundred yards before pulling off and dropping down onto Sackville Street, and entering the Gay Village passing the Rembrandt Hotel and bar then left into Bloom Street and finding somewhere to park.

My destination was the Hollywood Showbar, owned by Julia Grant who'd achieved fame through her "Change of Sex" TV series. I was heading for Concorde – a transvestite/ transsexual group that met downstairs on a Wednesday evening. I'd been a couple of times a few years before when it met upstairs at the Rembrandt but it had been rare for my business trips to allow an overnight stop near Manchester.

As I went down the stairs, I remembered the first time I'd tried to attend a trans meeting. That had been on Upper Street in Islington, London – probably 15 years or more earlier. I'd found the venue – an innocuous door that looked just like most of the others in the area. I'd walked past to carry out a recce, then back down the street, checking if anyone might be watching; wondering all the time what I'd find behind the door. What if it was a den of sex-mad perverts? Or Danny la Rue imitators in evening gowns and big wigs? Or all Tula look-alikes; she'd been the Bond girl from 'For Your Eyes Only' – who'd been outed as transsexual. How would I fit in? Would my appearance pass muster? The questions that night had been non-stop – and, in the end, I hadn't made it through the door at all. It had taken several more years before I'd had the opportunity, and courage, to open that door! As it happens, one of my fears had proved justified. Yvonne, who ran the club, commented quite rudely about my wig and roughly adjusted it for me.

Now, however, I had more confidence. I knew that these gatherings were often much more like a Women's Institute meeting than a wife-swopping party. Not that I'd ever been to either. For most, it was an opportunity to release their alter egos and chat with others who felt the same way.

Because I was driving, I ordered a Coke from the bar. I looked around the room but didn't see anyone I recognised apart from Janet and Mary, the organisers.

"Come and sit with us," called a brunette from a group at one of the tables. Pleased to be invited to join them, I walked over.

"I'm Joan, this is Belinda, Jackie and Michelle – is this your first time here?"

"Not quite, I've been a couple of times before but not for a while as I live near Cambridge". This wasn't quite true but I didn't want to reveal too much about my home life. "I'm Chris."

"Welcome anyway," said Belinda as I sat down. "So, what brings you to Manchester this time?"

I explained that I'd be running a project out near the airport and hoped I'd be able to get to the Village most weeks in future.

"Excellent, well lots of us go out later to other clubs around the Village – you're welcome to tag along if you like," remarked Jackie. "We'll certainly be heading to Naps – that's Napoleons – just up the road, we get in free whilst everyone else pays. We're the bait for some of their other clients."

"She means the tranny fuckers," added Michelle "but she's too polite to use that term; not like me. It's up to you whether you take up any offers – some do, some don't. But they have dancing upstairs with lots of mirrors and there's nothing a girl likes more than seeing herself in a mirror."

"Maybe next time," I replied, "I'd like to get my bearings first – I've also got an early meeting tomorrow so don't want to be too late tonight."

"No problem, we're here most weeks. Aren't we girls?"

"We certainly are," confirmed Joan, Jackie and Michelle – almost in unison.

"OK – let's mark your cards," continued Belinda.

"Over there, in the corner are the twin set and pearl brigade – they never go out round the Village. Most are married and straight, in fact, some come with their wives. By the bar are Gina and Steph – they'll certainly be in Naps later looking for business if you get my drift. You've met 'Mary-the-legs' and Janet the two organisers. Over by the window are Barbara, Frances and Kath; they're TS rather than TV – Barbara is post-op, Frances is due for surgery later this year and Kath has just started attending the GIC."

"You look confused," Joan remarked.

"Just a bit," I admitted.

Belinda offered me a Peter Stuyvesant cigarette and lit one for herself, then went on to explain "TS is transsexual –women trapped in men's bodies, TVs are transvestites like us – well, that's assuming that you are TV rather than TS; post-op means Barbara has had the sex change surgery."

"They prefer to refer to it as Gender Reassignment Surgery or GRS, but that's such a mouthful," Jackie interjected. "Pre-op is when they're waiting for surgery and the GIC is the Gender Identity Clinic – where they get treatment; unless they are going privately, of course."

I shook my head with the new information. "Ok – that makes it clear as mud."

Belinda glared at the others who'd interrupted her and picked up her recitation, "Now the pecking order is post-op TS at the top, pre-op just below them. Super-trannies come next – they've had breast enhancements but don't plan to have GRS, they often work at places like Funny Girls in Blackpool – we don't get many of them coming in here of course – though you might see some of them upstairs in the Showbar or in Naps. They tend to look down on us. Then you get the ordinary trannies – with different strata depending on how they dress."

"Drag artists and drag queens are different – they have no wish to pass at all – they parody females," added Joan.

"OK, Tranny 101 class is now over," concluded Michelle as she drained her glass and stubbed out her cigarette. 'Time we were off seeing what's going on elsewhere in the Village. You sure you won't join us?"

"Thanks – but maybe next time."

Chapter 6.   Two Pieces of Chicken and Fries
9th April 1997

Belinda was getting a drink when I arrived at the group the following week. As I joined her at the bar, she turned to me.

"Hi Chris, what are you drinking?"

I asked for a Coke.

We took our glasses over to the table where Jackie and Michelle were already ensconced.

"No Joan this evening?" I asked.

"She's got a date tonight with a guy she met in Napoleons last week. Apparently, they're going out to dinner but we might see them in there later."

I took a sip of my Coke and looked around. At first glance, it just seemed so ordinary; groups, mainly of women, having a drink and a chat. If an observer looked closer, they might notice that most of the women were wearing wigs and were taller than average; more than a few had strong jawlines with traces of five o'clock shadow and most spoke with deep voices.

"Penny for them."

I was brought back from my thoughts.

"Sorry, Michelle, I just can't get used to how normal it feels to be sitting here en-femme with all the other girls. Usually if I'm out dressed, I'm on edge expecting someone to make a comment or something worse."

"So, what do you usually do when dressed?" Jackie asked.

"Go for a drive, park up and have a walk somewhere secluded, maybe stop somewhere for a coffee. If I'm away on business, I might go to the cinema – hiding in the dark."

"Don't you go to gay clubs? Or meet others?"

"Apart from Concorde and a similar group in London, I haven't been anywhere. I've chatted to a few others online but not in person."

"What? You've never been to a club and danced the night away? Girl, have you got a treat waiting for you! Tonight, you're coming out with us and we won't take no for an answer – will we ladies?"

I'd hoped they'd invite me to join them again so didn't argue.

"Where are we heading for first this evening?" asked Jackie. "Paddy's Goose? New York New York? New Union? Dotz?"

"What do you fancy Chris? Paddy's is an Irish pub, New York New York and New Union have drag acts, Dotz is a piano bar with a singalong," Michelle told me.

"I'm not keen on drag acts but the piano bar sounds good. Do they let us in?"

"Hell, girl, this entire area is the Gay Village; there are a few places that cater for specific tastes but other than that, we get in anywhere. The Rem, that's the Rembrandt, is basically a gay men's venue; though, ironically, Concorde used to meet in the upstairs bar before moving here – but we'd never go in the main bar."

"Dotz it is then," said Belinda.

After a couple more drinks, we collected our coats from the cloakroom and climbed the stairs to the street.

"This is New York New York," Jackie remarked, as we passed a pub with music blaring out.

"Good evening, ladies. Coming in?" asked a bouncer on the door.

"Not tonight, darling," Jackie replied.

We crossed over the road and continued up the street. I was just amazed to be walking in a major city dressed en-femme with nobody taking any notice of us. We weren't even attracting any glances. I could get used to this.

"If you need a taxi, Village Cabs are here, just give your name to the guy on the door and where you're going. They get busy on a Saturday night and you can sometimes wait an hour or more after midnight, but they're safe for us," Michelle told me. "OK, Mo?" she said to a young Asian man standing with a clipboard in the doorway.

"Fine, Michelle. Are you going to need a cab later?"

"Yes please, put me down for about 1am."

At the corner a few yards further on, we turned right.

"This is Napoleons, we'll be coming here later. We get in free unless Clive thinks you're a real girl then you have to pay," Jackie said.

A shop with all manner of erotica in the windows of Clone Zone then caught my eyes as we passed. What on earth did you do with some of those items? I wondered.

"Here we are," Jackie said as we turned into the next narrow alley. Dotz piano bar was just across the road. A grey-haired fifty-something guy in a dinner jacket, wearing glasses, stood at the door but stepped aside as we approached.

Inside, about twenty customers gathered around a piano on a dais were singing along to 'American Pie'. The pianist waved one hand to our group and Jackie gestured with her hand to ask if he wanted a drink — which he answered with a nod and a blown kiss.

The next hour or so soon passed. Everyone just seemed to get on with enjoying themselves I couldn't remember having felt so relaxed and knew this would become one of my favourite venues. Even though I couldn't hold a tune — and my voice was deeper than I'd like — nobody gave a damn. Even in the toilets nobody cared. We were presenting as female and treated as such.

Eventually, though, Jackie looked at her watch and asked if we were ready to move on to Napoleons. I drank the last of my Coke and picked up my coat.

With a final wave to Tony the pianist and another to the barman, we said goodnight to Thomas on the door. Jackie had, by now, had a few drinks and was tottering on her five-inch heels. She did, however, make it the thirty or so yards to Napoleons.

"The dancing is upstairs," Michelle told me as Clive on the door let us in without charge. We made our way up the narrow stairs, hung our coats up then approached the bar. The heavy beat from the dance floor to our right had my feet tapping immediately.

"Hi, babes, what can I get you?" the blond barman asked.

"White wines for Jackie and Michelle, a Fosters for me and a glass of Coke for Chris, please Gary," said Belinda.

As Gary passed me my Coke, he said "Haven't seen you in here before, have we?"

I confirmed it was my first visit.

I realised I didn't really want to drink any more fizzy liquid at that moment and explored the dance floor. It wasn't that big, perhaps fifteen feet square, but was almost completely surrounded by mirrors. Several other TVs were dancing by themselves watching their reflections. I stepped onto the floor.

The sensation of my skirt swirling around my legs was incredible; wearing high heels, albeit only two-inch, changed my balance – forcing me onto the balls of my feet, rather than flat-footed as I would in male-mode and I let myself flow with the music. I'd thought that my outfit was appropriate at the group earlier – and hadn't seemed out of place in the piano bar but I had to admit that, compared with some of the other girls' outfits, mine was a bit dowdy. I could see a shopping trip beckoning. Of course, outfits that would be great for Naps wouldn't be appropriate for my normal outings and storing more clothes would pose a problem while I lived between home and the hotel.

Others had now joined the dance floor and a guy sidled up in front of me then turned to face me and matched my moves. When the music changed to a slow number, he put his hands on my hips and tried to pull me into his arms; I swivelled out of reach.

"I need a drink," I told him. He followed me to the bar and offered to pay for the Coke I ordered from Gary.

"I don't think I'm what you're looking for," I told him. "Dancing with you was fun but I'm not into guys." He shrugged his shoulders and walked away. I took my drink over to a bar stool next to the entrance to the dance floor and put my glass on a narrow shelf that ran along the wall while I hoisted myself onto a seat that seemed to have come off a vintage tractor.

I lit a cigarette and looked around the room. The décor was tired, the wallpaper peeling off in places, scratched paintwork, the carpet showing a clear sign of the path from the top of the stairs to the bar. The windows were covered in and the lighting came from a few red neon strips on the ceiling supplemented by flashes reflecting off the glitter ball above the dance floor escaping through the arch next to me. In daylight I was quite sure it would seem really tacky but right now it was Nirvana; a place I could be my alter ego; somewhere I'd already made friends who accepted me as Christine, where we didn't ask questions and just took folks for who they were.

Out on the dance floor, I could see Joan dancing very closely with her date; her arms around his neck and his hands fondling her bum. She was obviously enjoying herself and I felt jealous that she was comfortable expressing her female side to that extent.

"Enjoying yourself?" Belinda's question brought me out of my musing.

"Absolutely, so is Joan by the look of it," I replied with a laugh.

"Do I detect envy?"

"Not at all," I lied.

"Really?"

"No, I'm a happily married straight guy who cross-dresses. I've no interest in other men," I assured her.

"Not even the least bit curious about how it feels to have a guy treat you as a woman?"

I thought for a moment while I lit another cigarette. Would I ever want to do the same? Before tonight, I'd have said no. Now I wasn't quite so sure. Dancing earlier, I'd felt feminine and maybe I was curious about how it would feel to be held like Joan.

"Hey, don't look so shocked at the thought. Your female side is being released this evening – why shouldn't she want more?" Belinda added. "Just be careful, once you let the Genie out of the lamp, she won't want to go back in.

"Anyway, I came over to tell you that Michelle and I are popping round to McTucky's for something if you fancy a bite to eat."

I'd missed dinner while getting ready to come out, so joined them for two pieces of chicken and fries.

Chapter 7.   I'll have the Special
Thursday 17th July 1997

The next two months I spent Wednesdays and Thursdays in Manchester – travelling up on the Tuesday evening and back again late Thursday afternoon. Then the work started to build up and, by July, I found myself driving up on the Monday after a day in the office and returning Friday evening. I became a regular at the support group and got to know most of the other usual attendees.

Stopping in the hotel was becoming a bind though. It meant I had to keep all my female items hidden away from the cleaners during the day, carry the case to and from my car each trip – then hide it in the garage at home over the weekends. When it had been just one bag, it hadn't been too difficult but I'd bought extra dresses; well, I could hardly wear the same outfits to the group every week. I was also increasingly concerned about any of the staff recognising me going to and from my car when dressed – or even out around the Village. And there was the problem of laundering and drying my smalls and nightdresses.

I thought about renting a flat instead and discussed it with Ed. He had no problem with me doing so providing it saved the company money too. We negotiated a deal covering all accommodation and utility bills. Ed also specified that I had to look for the flat and organise moving in my own time and at my own expense.

It was easy enough finding a small flat within the budget; the problem was privacy. I could hardly tell the letting agents that I wanted somewhere that I could enter and leave without being seen. I was also concerned about the car and, ideally, wanted somewhere with off-road parking.

One of the flats I was offered was on the first floor of a modern development with pass controlled outer doors – but, when I viewed the property, it became apparent that my neighbour had little else to do but watch the comings and goings and would have been able to see me getting in and out of my car. Another was next door to a hall with a youth club whose members hung around outside and were a potential problem.

There seemed to be snags with everything I looked at and I was beginning to give up hope of finding somewhere suitable when I received details of a development that was about to become available. *'The property is part of a newly converted, treble-fronted, three-storey building with bay windows on the ground and first floors. Flat 1 is accessed through its own entrance to the side of the property.'* That caught my attention immediately.

The floor plan showed six flats in all in a building at the junction of Drake Avenue and Beech Road. The main entrance to the other flats was through a front door into a hall. The location, on the edge of Chorlton, was also ideal. I'd be driving the opposite way to most traffic to and from work and it was only another fifteen minutes into the Gay Village.

I immediately arranged a viewing for the Thursday afternoon – I reckoned I'd cone enough unofficial overtime in the evenings at the hotel to cover it.

I parked my car at the rear of the block. It was surrounded by an eight-foot-high wall. Each space was numbered; the one for flat 1 was under what would be the bedroom window. There was a single door with a security light above it about two-thirds of the way along the wall. It would be easy to get in and out of my car when dressed without being seen – especially if I removed the interior light bulb.

I looked around for the agent; he was just coming out of the door. He pasted a smile on his face as he approached me, his hand outstretched.

"Mr Williamson?" he enquired as I took his hand. "I'm Vince Walker from Harper and Harper. The entrance to Flat 1 is down here," he said, pointing along the path then stepping aside to allow me to precede him. "The other flats are through the door I came out of."

The path was hemmed between the building and the wall that surrounded the property. I knew, from the plans, the only windows on this side were for bathrooms. The door to flat 1 was inset into the wall, creating a porch. It meant I would be hidden even if anyone was leaning out of one of the windows which really wasn't likely – but I'd become used to assessing every possible risk. Opposite the door was a gate in the wall leading out onto Beech Road. Brilliant. I could even leave my car on the side road if I wanted to avoid using the car park during daylight.

Vince unlocked the door and led the way inside.

"The bathroom is here on the right," he informed me. I glanced in; a bath with a shower over it, toilet and basin confirmed what he'd said.

"And the bedroom is on the left," he continued.

The right-hand wall of the bedroom was taken up with a double bed and bedside cabinets; the opposite wall had fitted wardrobes either side of a dressing table. It was ideal. I immediately visualised being able to store Christine's clothes in one side of the wardrobe – with my drab male clothes in the other; I knew the dressing table would soon be covered with bottles of perfume, cosmetics, skin care products, stands for my jewellery and the like.

"The lounge has bay windows overlooking the front garden," Vince announced – though why he bothered stating the obvious, I don't know. A two-seater settee and armchair looked comfortable enough. I just hoped the lounge and dining room curtains Lucinda had replaced at home would be long enough – and wide enough – for the windows.

"And, as you can see, the kitchen dining area is well-appointed."

I supposed that was fair enough. The units were new, if bland; there was a reasonable cooker and a small fridge under the worktop. The small table and a couple of chairs were adequate for my needs.

All in all, I couldn't have designed a better layout. It was perfect. I'd need a few bits and pieces but a trip to Ikea or even a large supermarket would soon resolve most of that problem except for a TV and, of course, a hi-fi system. I do like my music. But I knew where I could get those.

"I'll take it," I told the agent and went back to their office to organise the paperwork. They did a credit check on line, the result of which, together with a letter from the company confirming my employment, satisfied them and I signed the lease there and then and handed over my debit card for them to take the deposit and first month's rent.

Then, it was back to the hotel to change and a celebratory meal in the Village – the 'specials' at the Blue Café were usually superb but Lisa, the chef, excelled herself that evening or maybe it was just my euphoria.

Chapter 8.   Fish and Chips
Friday 18th July 1997

On Friday, I left work after my conference call with head office and drove to a supermarket to pick up some essentials for the following week; then it was to the flat to drop off my bag of female clothes and the shopping. When I went to hang them up in the wardrobe, I realised there were no hangers. That was something else to add to the list I was making.

As I returned to my car, another resident pulled up. While I really didn't want to get too involved with my neighbours, it would have been rude to just drive off so I walked over and introduced myself before explaining that I had a long drive but I'd see him around.

Three hours later, I pulled up at a chippy in the village next to ours and purchased three fish suppers for dinner. Their cod or haddock and chips were acknowledged as the finest for miles around; the batter light and crunchy while the chips were soft on the inside but crispy on the outside. Lucinda would have plates warming in the oven and the table laid ready for my arrival.

I dropped my case in the hall and Lucinda took the carrier bag containing the fish and chips from me as soon as I entered the house. As usual, the dogs demanded attention but Olivia got in first.

"I wish you didn't have to work away so much, dad," she said as she hugged me.

I caressed her shoulder and ruffled her hair. "So do I, darling, but it's part of the job at the moment, I'm afraid."

We sat down at the table as Lucinda brought the loaded plates through to the dining room.

"So, what's this flat like?" she asked as she added vinegar and salt to her meal.

"Nice enough, one bedroom, a lounge, kitchen dinner and bathroom. It's a new renovation of a large Victorian house in a reasonable area in South Manchester. It's quite well equipped but I'll need to buy a few bits and pieces."

"Just one bedroom? So even if Olivia and I wanted to come up for a visit, there wouldn't be enough space?"

"Not really; unless Olivia slept in the lounge, unfortunately." God, that was the last thing I'd want. I'd have to sanitise the place if they were to come. "Not that there's much for you there anyway. If you wanted a weekend away or something, there are better places to go."

"So, what are you going to need for the flat?" Lucinda asked as she finished the last of her chips.

"Bedding, kitchen utensils, pots and pans, a kettle. I thought I could take the old curtains and cushions."

"Those old things? Well, yes, take them if you want, but I thought you said the flat was furnished?"

"Part furnished," I clarified. "The main furniture is there and a cooker and fridge – but not soft furnishings and the like."

"And you're planning to move in when you go back on Monday?"

"Yes, I can pick up some essentials after work – there's a big superstore near the office that will have most of what I need. I could also take some of our camping cooking things to keep me going initially."

"Mum called yesterday; she was asking when we're going to visit them." Lucinda's parents lived in Hastings. I got on well enough with them but the idea of another couple of hours' drive on a Friday evening really didn't appeal to me. "The summer break starts on Friday. I thought of taking Olivia down to see them for a week. I know you wouldn't want to spend that long with them but it would give you the chance to stay at the flat over the weekend and get it sorted out."

"Are you sure your parents won't mind me not going? It would make things easier for me," I replied, trying to keep a straight face though my heart was thumping. It would mean I could spend a whole weekend as Christine and get to visit the Village on a Saturday night; in fact, even Friday AND Saturday nights.

Chapter 9.   Dinner Date
Friday 25th July 1997

I finished work at lunchtime on Friday and returned to the flat via the supermarket. Undressing, I bundled my male things into the laundry basket del ghting with the idea that I wouldn't be using them again for sixty-five hours. I laid out my feminine undies, a blouse and summery skirt and my nightdress for later then had a shower using J'Adore gel rather than the pine-scented one I used in male mode. I slipped on a floral kimono bathrobe after my bath while I did my make-up.

A little over an hour later, I was nearly ready to leave. I checked my handbag and made sure I had my credit card. When I'd applied for a separate card to use for business expenses, I had a second one in Lucinda's name – it meant I could present Mr C Williamson in male mode and Mrs C Williamson when presenting as Christine. In either case, the signature on the reverse was 'Chris Williamson'. I slipped on a pair of low-heeled sandals as I'd heard how much walking was involved in a trip to Ikea, which I'd decided was the best place to get most of what I needed.

Lucinda usually had firm ideas about anything she bought for the home – typically based on latest trends in style magazines. It wasn't always what I liked but it was easier to leave it to her. This time it was different. This time, the look would be 'Christine's'.

I hadn't planned to buy any wall art – but two pictures caught my attention and I knew immediately where I was going to hang them. The first was a landscape with mountains in the background shrouded in mist surrounding a fiord. In the foreground, a rock jutted out over the void with a tiny image of a woman sitting on the extremity, her feet over the edge. It spoke of someone at peace with herself; a fantastic view in front of her – but danger in her position. If that didn't describe my situation, I didn't know what would. I knew it would be the focal point in the lounge.

The second was a girl's face emerging from a garland of pink and red roses in an ethereal look. It was perfect for the bedroom and I'd seen matching duvet and pillow set and curtains that would go perfectly and create the feminine feel I was looking for. Burgundy globe-shaped lights with self-coloured shades would be just right for the bedside cabinets and I'd seen ceiling lampshades in the same shade. It was definitely coming together.

By the time I got to the tills, the trolley was overflowing not just with the items that had been on my list but another dozen or so essentials I hadn't realised I needed. Back at the flat, I unpacked the bedroom furnishings, hung the curtains and made the bed. The portrait of the girl with the garland of flowers added the finishing touch. But God help me if Lucinda did ever pay me a visit; this was definitely not a male bedroom.

The rest of the unpacking could wait. I had another shower before dressing in a shortish (for me) black dress. I poured myself a glass of wine while I redid my make-up ready for a chance to explore the Village on a Friday evening then I called for a cab, which arrived a few minutes later and waited outside the gate on Beech Road.

"Where to, darling?" the driver enquired, his eyes dropping to my stocking-clad legs.

"Sackville Street, please," I told him. Maybe it was my voice or maybe it was my destination but his eyes widened as he raised his glance from my legs to my face.

"Oh. Right, mate," he said.

He dropped me opposite the Blue Café and I entered my favourite eatery in the Village. Tonight's special was a lamb dish with rice which I had with another glass of wine. As always it was fabulous. Saying goodnight to Lisa, the chef, I made my way across Sackville Street to Dotz.

"Hi Chris, don't normally see you in here at the weekend. Usual Coke?" asked the barman.

"No, I'll have a glass of white wine tonight, please," I said. He raised his eyebrows in surprise. "I'm not driving tonight," I explained.

"Right, is Chardonnay OK?" It was.

An hour or so later, I drained my fourth or was it my fifth glass of wine that evening, said my goodnights and walked along the road to Napoleons. Belinda and Jackie were just about to enter as I reached the door so we went in together, waved through by Clive.

We made our way to the upstairs bar where both Gary and Colin were busy serving. Although we'd only just arrived, Gary asked what we wanted to the annoyance of a couple of the guys already waiting. It paid to be recognised as regulars.

I chatted with Belinda and Jackie for a few minutes before The Macarena started to play. I joined the others on the dance floor as we did the moves; it was followed by YMCA then the Timewarp and Barbie Girl. When the cheesy numbers gave way to other tunes, a guy stepped in front of me and we danced together.

I remembered the previous time this had happened and how I'd been jealous of Joan's intimacy with her date. Whether it was the wine or just the thrill of being Christine that had suppressed my inhibitions; this time, when the music slowed and the guy put his hands around my waist and pulled me closer, I slipped my arms around his neck and rested my head on his shoulder. It felt absolutely natural. When he fondled my bum, I pressed closer to him. I felt him nibbling my ear and I lifted my head from his shoulder. He looked into my eyes then tilted his head slightly. I knew what was coming; but what would it be like to kiss a guy? I remembered what Belinda had said last time about my femme alter ego being let loose.

His lips brushed mine and I responded. He pressed harder and I let his tongue slip into my mouth. Our tongues entwined and I felt my body shiver. It was incredible. Belinda and her dance partner had manoeuvred close to me. She gave me a wink and whispered: "Enjoy it, girl." I intended to.

After a few more dances, my partner asked if I'd like a drink. He held my hand as we walked over to the bar. While he ordered the drinks, I had a chance to appraise him. Even in my heels, he was a couple of inches taller than me, slim but not skinny, probably late forties early fifties, quite distinguished looking with well-groomed hair. He was wearing a rugby shirt with horizontal green and red stripes and a white collar over Chinos and leather shoes – not trainers.

"There you go, darling. I'm Philip, by the way."

I told him my name as he offered me a cigarette then gave me a light.

"Well, cheers," he said holding his glass for me to clink mine against. We both took sips of the wine. He then put his glass on the ledge around the room and leant towards me. As we kissed again, I wondered how far Philip would want to go – and how far I'd be prepared to go. His hand rested on my knee then slid a bit higher. I was torn. I really wanted to explore further but was scared that if I did, it would take me places I wasn't ready for. What had Belinda said about genies and bottles?

I sat up.

"I'm really sorry Philip but I'm not sure I'm ready for anything more tonight."

He squeezed my hand. "That's OK darling, I understand but will you have dinner with me tomorrow night? Please, I think you're fabulous and I'd love to get to know you better."

I wasn't sure. Could I continue to resist him if we met again? Would I, if I could?

"Look, put my number in your phone. If I don't hear from you, I'll assume we'll meet for dinner tomorrow evening – or shall I pick you up?"

I certainly wasn't ready to give him my address. And I could always cancel the date so I agreed to meet him outside Taurus about eight-thirty the following evening. With that, I told him I was going to get a cab home. He walked with me round to Village cabs then pulled me into a doorway once I'd given Mo my details.

Eventually, Mo called "Chris. Next one is yours" as one of the taxis drew up. Philip and I broke apart from our clinch.

"Are you sure I can't come with you?"

"No, Philip. Now let me go. I'll see you tomorrow evening."

Back at the flat, I kicked off my heels poured another glass of wine and sat at my dressing table while I lit a cigarette and cleaned and moisturised my face. What was I going to do? Should I meet Philip tomorrow? I could still taste his lips on mine in spite of having brushed my teeth; I could still feel his arms around me. That night I dreamt of him taking my breasts in his hands and teasing my nipples and kissing and nibbling them; of him fondling me between my legs before penetrating.

I woke six hours later and made a mug of instant coffee and some toast under the grill. I was surprised I didn't have a hangover having drunk at least a bottle and a half of wine last night. So, was I going on a date with Philip this evening or not? I didn't actually need to decide yet. I was certainly going out somewhere this evening and I had a lot to do before then.

After breakfast, I drove to a large electrical store and collected a trolley from the rack outside. I selected a vacuum cleaner, coffee filter machine, toaster and microwave then made my way to the display of televisions. I looked around for an assistant – but, as usual, they were chatting to each other. Eventually, I caught the eye of a young lad emerging from a door at the back of the store. When he reached me, I was standing next to a display of flat-screen televisions.

"Are you looking for anything in particular? These flat screen TVs are going to be the future," he assured me. At just under £1,000 it would be a long way in the future for me. I settled for a normal 26inch model and a video recorder. As Christopher, I could have carried the TV with ease– as Christine, I wasn't going to try carrying it – it might have attracted attention.

"I'm also after a washing machine and tumble drier," I told him. I think I saw his eyes light up at the thought of more commission. He led the way across the store leaving me to push the trolley.

I arranged for the larger items to be delivered on the Monday; I wouldn't normally be expected in the office until late morning in any case. The smaller items, I loaded in the car. Next on my list was an outfit for this evening. If I was going on a date with Philip, I wanted a new dress. What did I mean IF? Who was I kidding?

I parked near Trafford Bar tram stop and was soon in the city centre. It was exciting looking for a dress for a special date; trying to find exactly the right outfit. The problem was that I couldn't go for anything low-cut at the front as I didn't have the natural attributes to produce a cleavage and I hated showing any of my bra – let alone the falsies I needed to use to fill it. I did, eventually, find a sleeveless, boat-necked, knee-length skater dress in a gorgeous Persian blue with crimson roses running in a curve across the skirt from the hem and up onto one of the breasts. Having found the dress, I needed shoes and a handbag to go with it. What about matching bra though? I didn't want black straps showing through and if I had a blue bra, the panties had to match too. Fortunately, I managed to find the latter in Debenhams. The coordinated items included suspender belt which I'd need as well and I bought some barely black stockings to complete the outfit.

It was nearly five o'clock by the time I got back to the flat. I unpacked my purchases, hung the dress up and laid the undies out on the bed. I then rang my parents-in-law's house in Hastings for a chat with Lucinda and Olivia. It felt a bit incongruous speaking to them while laying on my bed in a skirt and blouse. Duty done, I ran a bath laced with J'Adore bath gel. While it filled, I poured a glass of wine to drink while I soaked. I lit a cigarette and closed my eyes breathing in the scent from the bubble bath.

The full-length mirror I'd bought at Ikea was still leaning against the wall, but I could check my appearance. Not bad, even if I did say so myself. The dress looked and felt absolutely gorgeous. The high-heels were a little higher than I normally wore but were spot on.

My phone rang to say the taxi was outside so I walked out to the road. As we reached the Mancunian Way, I realised I was going to be a few minutes late; but that was a woman's prerogative, wasn't it? Even so, as the driver filtered off the fly-over, I sent Philip a text saying "On my way be with you soon C xx"

He replied with "Can't wait to see you xxx"

The driver dropped me at the top of Canal Street and I saw Philip standing there waiting for me.

I felt a frisson in my stomach as I saw his smile. He took me in his arms and kissed me.

"I've been dreading all day getting a text from you saying you weren't going to come. You look absolutely fabulous. That dress suits you so well. It highlights your blue eyes." He kissed me again before wrapping his arm round my waist as he led me into Taurus.

We were shown to a table and given menus. "There are some specials on the blackboard as well," the waitress informed us. "Can I get you something to drink while you decide what you're having?"

"Chardonnay?" Philip suggested. I nodded my agreement.

"A bottle, please," he told the waitress.

I took out my cigarettes and offered him one. He looked at me and said, "You really do look lovely, my God, I want to just look at you."

I took a drag on my cigarette and blew the smoke towards the ceiling then lowered my eyes to look into his.

"Is that all you want to do?"

"You know damned well it's not, you minx. But I've promised not to pressure you and I'll stick to that promise."

"Thanks, love," I replied. "To be honest, I don't know what I want. Half of me wants to say 'take me back to your place and fuck me silly'. The other half is scared stiff of starting something I won't be able to stop. Last night was the first time I'd even kissed a guy. It was incredible. You're incredible. But I'm married and have a daughter and I don't want to risk anything that will hurt them. Can you understand?"

"Absolutely. I assume they don't know anything about you cross-dressing?"

"No. They don't. They don't even know I smoke. So, maybe another secret doesn't really make much difference." It was a place I didn't really want to think about so I picked up the menu. "What do you recommend?" I asked.

Over dinner, Philip told me he was a manager in the health service working in one of the main hospitals in Manchester, he had a town house in Hulme, had been married but was now divorced and had a son and daughter that he rarely saw. I'd revealed a lot more than I'd planned – but he was so easy to talk to. We seemed to laugh at the same jokes; and when 'Sweet Caroline' started to play in the background, we simultaneously said we loved Neil Diamond's music.

"I saw him in concert last year, here in Manchester," Philip told me. I was so jealous.

"I'd love to see him, but Lucinda isn't really into him. She still sees him as the wild man on the cover of Hot August Night. But I'll be getting some of his records for the flat."

"Have you heard his collection 'In my Lifetime'? It was released last year. I've got it on CD, you'll have to come and listen to it." He held up his hands. "And, that's all I'm suggesting. If you want to leave after you've listened to it, I won't stop you."

I rested my hand on his.

"That's so sweet. I'd love to," I told him.

Walking down the cobbles of Canal Street, we held hands and I drank in the intoxicating atmosphere. When Philip pulled me into his arms, I slipped mine around his neck and responded to his kiss – a moan escaping from my throat as my body reacted to his caresses. We went into Via Fosse where I tried to insist on paying for our drinks – but Philip wouldn't hear of it. He guided me to one of the upper levels and we found a private booth. I rested my hand on his knee and he slid his arm around my shoulders and tilted my head to his. His other hand gently took mine and placed it on his bulge as his tongue played with mine. I traced the outline of his cock try ng to gauge just how big t was. If it was anything like the rest of this guy, it would be impressive.

Oh shit, where was this going to lead?

Did how I was feeling mean I was gay, or at least bisexual? As a male, I had never had the slightest attraction to other men. But it was as though I was Christine at the moment and it felt so right. Could Christine have an affair without it impacting on Christopher? How far did things have to go before it became an affair? Was this already an affair? Would it be any more serious if I did have sex with Philip? Would I regret it if I did?

Philip's hand had now released mine and was creeping up under my skirt. His kisses became even more passionate and more moans escaped from my lips. His fingers slipped inside my panties and wrapped around my own penis. As he stroked the end, my breathing became heavier. It felt so good. But it also reminded me that I was a guy and that didn't feel right. I sat up, picked up my glass and took a drink. Philip did the same then offered me a cigarette.

"Sorry, I went too far, didn't I?" he asked.

I took a drag on my cigarette while I thought about it.

"I just don't know. I loved everything we were doing; it just feels right while Christine is dominant but when you touched my prick, it reminded me that I wasn't really female and the i lusion was lost. Sorry."

"So, if I hadn't done that, you were quite happy? You didn't mind fondling me?"

"No, because what I was doing was normal for a woman. Does that sound silly?"

"Not at al , I'll just have to bear it in mind next time and avoid touching you there – if there's going to be a next time."

Did I want there to be a next time?

Philip's arm was still around my shoulder. I felt him starting to lift it from me but I put my hand on his and held it there. He gave me a quizzical look and I smiled and tilted my head towards him. As we kissed, I put my hand back on his cock and he cupped my left breast. Despite it being false, I could still feel the fondling.

"If you're going to keep doing that, darling, I think we'd be better off in private or I'm going to make an awful mess," he told me.

I looked him in the eyes; "Perhaps we should go and listen to some Neil Diamond then," I suggested

It was only just after eleven, so we had no problem getting a cab and were at Philip's after a short drive. The properties were new-looking three-storey 'upside down' townhouses with tiny front gardens behind low brick walls.

"The sitting room is on the top floor," Philip commented as he opened the door and let me enter.

As we reached the first floor, he pointed out the loo.

"Just come on up when you're ready," he said.

Two bedrooms led off the landing and I peeked inside each of them before taking the stairs up to the lounge. The lighting had been turned down and there was a bottle of sparkling wine and two glasses on the coffee table in front of a black leather sofa. Philip was putting CDs into a player linked to an expensive looking hi-fi system.

"Hope you're not in a hurry, darling, the total length of the tracks is nearly four hours."

"Well, if I don't get to hear them all this evening, I'll just have to come back for the rest, won't I?"

I sat down on the sofa and took the glass of fizz Philip offered and we lit cigarettes. I snuggled up to him. His right arm was wrapped around my neck and his hand was resting on my breast. The music was fabulous and I closed my eyes and just chilled; taking the occasional sip of wine and drag on my cigarette. Once I'd finished my cigarette, he took my glass from me and put it on the coffee table and we kissed. I put my hand on his thigh then moved it higher and stroked his penis through his Chinos. I found the zip and opened his fly. His tongue slid in and out of my mouth urgently. My fingers found the waistband of his pants and drew it down. My own breathing was now heavy with anticipation. Philip undid the button holding his waistband closed then lifted his bottom so I could pull his trousers and pants down.

I felt the back of my dress being unzipped and I let him lift it over my head before we settled back into our previous positions. Philip slipped my bra strap down, pulled the cup away from my chest and teased my nipples with his fingertips. As I fondled his penis, I felt my body shivering in response. I swear we were trying to eat each other as our tongues entwined. Then Philip pulled away and took my nipple between his teeth. Oh My God. It was incredible. But I forced him off as I had other plans while I was so highly aroused. I lowered my lips to his penis and kissed the tip then opened my mouth and took it inside.

"Jesus, Chris, that was incredible," he said as I lay with my head in his lap my legs stretched out on the sofa after we'd cleaned ourselves up. His fingers were fondling my nipples and he lifted my head to let me take a sip of wine from the glass he was holding in his other hand. He kissed my lips so very gently. "Thank you," he said.

I smiled at him. "Anytime, darling."

The music continued playing as we just lay there taking the occasional kiss. When '*Girl, You'll be a Woman Soon*' started to play, Philip stood up and held out his hand, pulled me to my feet and took me in his arms and sang along with Neil, looking straight into my eyes. I guessed what he meant and knew I was ready for it too. As the tune faded, I kissed him. I recognised the next track '*You got control*' from the opening bars. I pulled away, pointed at him and sang along – submitting to him. I lowered my eyes demurely and held out my hand. He took it and led me down the stairs to his bedroom.

I sat on the edge of the bed and Philip stood in front of me, his penis already fully erect. He pressed my shoulders back onto the bed then lifted my legs onto it spreading them apart then laying down on top of me. I could feel his erection pressing against my stomach as we kissed. Philip started to rub his cock against me as though he was inside me. I closed my eyes and imagined that I did, indeed, have a vagina that he was penetrating. My arms were round his back and I dug my nails into his skin. He pressed his lips hard against mine and plunged his tongue in and out of my mouth in time with his pelvic thrusts. I could feel tension building through my whole body.

Then he rocked back on his heels. He rolled a condom onto his cock. I lay there in anticipation. Could I take him? How much would it hurt? Could I go through with it?

Predicting my concerns, Philip told me not to worry, he'd be gentle. He handed me a small bottle. "Here, take a sniff of this."

"What is it?" I asked.

"Poppers – it'll help relax your sphincter"

I felt Philip pulling my knickers to one side and spreading lubricant into my anus as I did as he suggested. He then lifted my ankles over his shoulder and I felt him probing. He then slapped my bum and I tensed then relaxed. He slipped inside with only the slightest discomfort. He paused then pressed further.

"OK?" he asked.

"Fine," I told him – and it was.

He gradually built up the tempo, varying the pace to take us to the edge then backing off again. Then I felt him come and he collapsed on top of me.

He rolled to one side then stood up. "Be right back," I heard him climbing the stairs then coming back down. When he came back into the bedroom, he was holding the bottle of wine and glasses and our cigarettes.

We sat next to each other on top of the bedclothes, drinking and smoking. I was silent, lost in my thoughts. Where did this now leave me? Obviously, I had to hide tonight's activities from Lucinda and Olivia. Did I regret it happening? No, I didn't regret it. Did I feel guilty? To some extent

– but so long as what happened in Manchester stayed in Manchester, I could live with it.

I saw Philip watching me, a concerned look on his face.

"Having regrets?"

"No, definitely not. That was fucking incredible – incredible fucking even."

I turned my head and we kissed again.

I swung my legs off the bed and went into the en-suite bathroom. The face staring back at me in the mirror looked very satisfied. When I came out, I fetched my dress and handbag from the lounge and started to repair my make-up and put my dress on.

"What are you doing? Aren't you staying the night?"

"I'd love to but I can't. I don't have any other clothes with me and can hardly go home in this dress in the morning." My beard growth would also start to come through by then and I'd need to shave.

"I could drop you back to your place in the morning."

"I don't have all my make-up either."

"Well, I could lend you enough male clothes to get home in."

"Sorry, darling – but absolutely not. You know what happened when you touched my dick. I have to be Chr stine one hundred per cent when I'm with you or it won't work."

"So, when can I see you again then? Are you free tomorrow night?"

"I am, but I've got some deliveries due any time after eight on Monday morning so   still wouldn't be able to stay the night. We could still meet up though. If you want to. I do have to sort out stuff around the flat. But I could come over in the evening."

"Why don't we have a takeaway then? You can finish listening to the CDs." I was sure that wasn't all he intended to continue – at least, I hoped it wasn't.

I wrapped my arms around his neck and we kissed. I felt him starting to unzip my dress again and I swivelled out of his arms. "Save it for tomorrow. Now will you please call me a taxi?"

"Had a good evening, darling," enquired the taxi driver.

"Oh yes, best ever," I told him as I settled in my seat for the journey back to the flat.

Chapter 10. Takeaway for Two
Sunday 27th July 1997

My first thoughts, waking up on Sunday, were about Philip; the passion of our kisses, the excitement of our love-making; passion and excitement that had been lost from relations with Lucinda which had become kind of stale. Things between us had gone much further than I'd ever planned. Philip wasn't, of course, any competition for Lucinda. We were married and I loved her. Didn't I? Perhaps it was more accurate to say that we were comfortable together and shared common aims in life.

With Philip, it was pure lust – or maybe it was forbidden fruit tasting sweeter.

Perhaps I should feel guilty being unfaithful to Lucinda – but it really didn't seem like that. It was Christine who'd gone to bed with Philip and planned to do so again later – not Christopher. They were two separate worlds. Maybe they'd collide at some time in the future but, for now, I'd do my damndest to keep them apart.

I went into the kitchen and filled the coffee machine then had a shower while it filtered through. Wrapped in an aubergine towelling bathrobe, fastened on the female side I poured a mugful and lit a cigarette then checked my phone. I'd switched it off once I'd met Philip last night. I saw there was a message from Lucinda; as I dialled her number, I hoped there wasn't a problem with Olivia.

"Where were you last night?" Lucinda demanded when I got through.

"Sorry, as I haven't got a TV at the flat yet, I went out to the cinema," well not that kind of TV I thought, "I switched the phone off and forgot to switch it back on afterwards."

"Oh, I see. What was the film?"

"Mission Impossible, Tom Cruise. I knew it wasn't your sort of thing."

"Anyway, the thing is, Olivia's been invited to a birthday event next Saturday, it's for the daughter of mum's neighbours. You remember Charlene, don't you? They're going pony trekking. It means we won't be back next weekend though. Would you mind?"

Would I mind? My stomach fluttered at the thought of another weekend in Manchester and the opportunities it presented.

I heard "Let me speak to Dad," from Olivia and the phone at the other end was passed to her.

"Dad, please say you don't mind. I know we won't have seen you for three weeks but I really want to go pony trekking. Please," she pleaded.

"Of course you can go, darling," I told her. "I'll miss you too." And I would. But even if there hadn't been alternative attractions for me in Manchester, my reply would have been the same — what dad can't be twisted around his daughter's little finger?

"Thanks, Dad, mwaaaah, love you," she said as I heard Lucinda asking for the phone again.

"You really don't mind?"

"No, of course not — sounds like a lot of fun for Olivia," I assured her.

"Good. Well, must dash, we're going to Holy Communion at St Mary's and mum hates being late."

I poured another mug of coffee and lit another cigarette while I reviewed what I needed to do. There were quite a few items on the list including assembling the TV/hi-fi stand I'd bought at Ikea ready for the television and video recorder being delivered the next morning. I also wanted to go out and get a music system; that would then need setting up. Then I needed to hang the other pictures and the mirror. Better get moving then.

I dressed in a knee-length denim skirt, peasant-style top and sandals with a one-inch heel. I was much more proficient with my make-up now and, instead of taking nearly an hour as I used to, I took less than fifteen minutes. Then it was on with the wig and I was ready to go. Checking my appearance in the full-length mirror, I wondered if I would ever want to be female full-time. God, I hoped not. The price was just too high.

The assistant in the hi-fi systems shop seemed surprised that I was as interested in the total harmonic distortion and wow and flutter of the amplifier and tape player as in the styling and could discuss what I wanted in terms of watts RMS per channel output – but I was able to select what I wanted including speakers for the lounge and bedroom. If I'd gone there as Christopher, it would have been a different conversation, I was sure.

It was mid-afternoon before I'd assembled the cabinet – actually reading the instructions rather than assuming I knew what went where, connected the various components and tested the system. I put on the music while I hung the other pictures and the mirror and sorted out the remaining purchases from Ikea. With everything put away, I wandered around the flat. I was more than happy with the feel I'd created.

I took another mug of coffee into the lounge and smoked another cigarette before I ran a bath and prepared for my date with Philip. It was, unfortunately, necessary to shave; it was one masculine activity I couldn't avoid. Maybe I should consider electrolysis? The only time I'd had a moustache and beard was during a purge period when I started going out with Lucinda. I'd thought the cross-dressing was behind me. She preferred the smooth shaved look so I got rid of them. It would certainly simplify doing my make-up. For now, though, it was a very necessary evil. Fortunately, I had very little hair on my arms and legs and none on my chest.

Walking into my bedroom, I sat at the dressing table, pulled my hair back from my face and went through my routine. I'd taken my wig off while bathing so put it back on and brushed it into shape. Satisfied with the result, I slipped off the Kimono and wedge-heeled mules I'd been wearing and pulled on my bra and panties.

Concealing my penis was always a problem. I'd heard of some trans people 'tucking'; pushing their testicles back up inside the body and pulling the penis backwards and holding it in place with surgical tape – but I wasn't brave enough to even try that. I knew there were devices you could wear that hid the penis and claimed to allow you to sit and pee like a woman. Some had what they described as a realistic Venus mound and outer labia lips. I was sceptical about how effective they'd be, particularly about the claims that they had a cavity that allowed penetrative sex. Before last night, I hadn't even considered buying one as they cost hundreds of pounds. But, after last night, maybe it would be worthwhile.

Now, what should I wear? Skirt and blouse or a dress? Not the same as last night obviously, nor Friday. Hmm. I think I needed to do some more clothes shopping. I settled for a navy-blue button-through short-sleeved shirt dress. I decided to go bare-legged and slipped my feet into the sandals I'd worn to Ikea. Was it only two days ago? I'd painted my toenails on the Tuesday evening and they still looked fine. I clipped on a pair of drop earrings and a matching silver necklace with blue pendant. I wished I could get my ears pierced but that would be too noticeable.

Closing the door behind me, I walked up the path and through the gate to the car park. No one else was around so I slipped into the driving seat and drove out onto the main road. At a set of traffic lights, a Fiesta pulled alongside me and started to rev his engine. It sounded as though he'd put a two-inch exhaust pipe on the back to sound throatier. The driver looked about 23 and wore his baseball cap back to front. I knew what he was thinking seeing a 'bird' in a BMW. He would try to out-accelerate me. I could have left him standing but it just wasn't worth it. I let him go, belching clouds of black smoke then pulled up alongside him at the next lights. He looked over at me and smiled. Sweet Jesus did he seriously think I could be interested?

About half a mile from Philip's, I stopped at a Chinese take-away and bought our dinner.

As it was the weekend, there was no restriction on parking so I pulled up outside Philip's gate. I checked my lipstick in the mirror, slipped my bag over my shoulder, picked up the carrier bag containing the takeaway and got out. As I reached his door, it opened.

"Let me have that," he said taking hold of the bag. He leant towards me and we kissed hungrily. "First things first," Philip said "or the food will go cold". I hadn't eaten anything since breakfast so didn't argue. The living area and kitchen were lit by candles and Neil Diamond was playing again in the background as we sat down at the dining table.

We took our coffees into the lounge area after we'd eaten and sat together on the sofa while we smoked an after-dinner cigarette. Philip then took me in his arms. His lips touched mine, his tongue gently probed; I sucked it into my mouth. I felt his fingers undoing the top buttons of my dress and his hand sliding inside my bra to fondle my nipple. I moaned with delight and sought out his penis. He took my hand and stood up. "We'll be more comfortable downstairs," he said – and I wasn't going to argue.

Once in the bedroom, I sat on the edge of the bed and he came and stood in front of me. I undid his belt and his trousers dropped to the floor. I hooked my fingers into the waistband of his pants and peeled them down. His cock sprang to attention in front of my face; I took hold of it and took it in my mouth then gripped his arse cheeks while he slid it in and out. I could smell the masculine talc he must have used.

He withdrew, cupped my chin, lifted me to my feet, tilted my head back, kissed me forcibly and undid a few more buttons of my dress. He slipped it off my shoulders and it fell to the floor.

"Turn round," he said, "and lie down on the bed." He spread my legs apart and knelt between them. I felt my panties being pulled to one side and his finger teasing my anus. He sat up and there was a pause before I felt the coldness of lubricant around and in my hole then his cock entering. He lay on top of me and nuzzled my neck. His hands reached underneath me and played with my nipples as he gently penetrated. I desperately wanted to feel his lips on mine but couldn't for the moment. He built up the tempo of his thrusts bringing me close to the edge as well.

Then, with a few final firm plunges, he slumped on top of me. The pressure on my prostate eased as he became limp and, after a few moments, he rolled off me. I turned over and leant on his chest and fastened my lips onto his. I was still so hungry for him. Eventually, we decoupled, Philip passed me a cigarette and held my hand as we lay there smoking.

I reflected that three months ago, I'd pulled away from a guy who'd tried to kiss me. Friday evening I'd let Philip kiss me and I was now comfortable having sex with him – providing my own penis wasn't involved. I turned on my side and kissed him softly and rested my hand on his prick. I felt it respond.

"Mmmm," I purred, stroking it as our kiss became more urgent. I continued to fondle him as I kissed his chin then his chest, nibbled his nipples then made my way further down his abdomen. I got between his legs and lowered my head onto his member.

"Come here, darling," he said pulling my arms. I shuffled up his torso and he took my nipples between his teeth – alternating them. My body started to shake. I could see the packet of condoms on the bedside table and took one out and shuffled back down so I could roll it onto him. Then I squatted over him and lowered myself onto his stiff prick. I groaned each time I sank down onto him and he stretched me. He thrust upwards to meet me and we gradually increased the length of each stroke and the speed until I felt him offload.

"Fuck me," I sighed as I collapsed on him.

"I think I just did," he said. "Can't you stay the night?"

"Not tonight sweetheart – but I could next weekend," I explained that Lucinda and Olivia wouldn't be home that weekend so I'd be in Manchester.

Chapter 11. Cherry Picking
Wednesday 30th July 1997

Wednesday I was back at Concorde. I'd made friends with a lot of the members by now. They were certainly a mixed crowd; the twinset and pearl brigade, as Belinda had described them, were far from as stuffy as they'd seemed initially and I'd had a few chats with a couple of the wives. I really wished Lucinda could be as understanding as some of them. But that wasn't ever going to happen.

Talking to Frances, Barbara and Kath, the transsexual members, had been an eye-opener. I'd been aware that it was possible to have treatments to modify the body using hormones and having surgery – but I hadn't realised what they had to go through to get that treatment or the time it could take. Shit, what a palaver. Thankfully I didn't see myself going down that route. I was quite happy with what I had – though having real boobs to create a cleavage would be fabulous.

Gina and Steph were an interesting couple. Some of the other members shunned them because of their sex work. I suspected they came into the group because they knew it pissed off some of the others. They really didn't need what Concorde could provide – they were, it seemed, quite happy doing their own thing quite openly. They certainly didn't need the changing facilities – they had a flat off Waterloo Road where they entertained the guys they picked up in Napoleons and, if rumours were to be believed, they had a dungeon for guests who enjoyed S&M. Personally, I didn't see the attraction of bondage but each to their own. Tonight, Gina was wearing a black corset which barely covered her, obviously enhanced, breasts over a very short leather miniskirt that gave glimpses of her knickers every time she bent over or crossed her fishnet-clad legs. Her thigh-high boots must have been painted on; it was the only explanation for how they fitted; and how she managed those five-inch stiletto heels, I'll never know. I struggle enough with three-inch heels.

As the pair of them left the club, probably for New York, New York, Val, Krystal's wife, beckoned to me to join them.

"What do you make of that pair?" she asked.

"It's not my style and it's not the life I'd want," I said, "but I guess they've got to earn a living somehow and it's their bodies. Not easy getting a job if you're transsexual. If you're TV you can usually hide it, but God help you if it comes out. Krystal is so lucky to have you. I can't see my wife accepting it."

"It took a lot of soul searching," Val said, "I didn't like it when I first found out. I worried what family, friends and neighbours would say. But I didn't want to lose Colin the man and Krystal was part of that deal so there you go. I'm not sure I'd have been quite as accepting, though, if he'd kept it hidden until we'd been married instead of telling me before we got engaged."

"That's understandable. I thought it was just a phase I'd gone through and I was over it when I proposed. I think, though, it was more that I was focussed on my relationship with Lucinda at the time and my transvestism had been suppressed."

"Common tale, isn't it Krystal?" said Val.

"It is. We hear it all the time. So, you wouldn't consider coming out to Lucinda, is it?" Krystal asked.

"Yes, Lucinda. The problem is, she has solid middle-England attitudes. Oh, she'll laugh at Lilly Savage and Dame Edna on television but she makes derogatory remarks about gay men and any transvestites she reads about in her magazines or in the News of the World. Then there's her church. I consider myself a believer – but her evangelical minister cherry-picks phrases from the Bible. Or maybe that's just me trying to excuse my cross-dressing which I know is one of those areas he claims the Bible regards as an abomination."

"We know what you mean. Don't we, Krystal. It's ironic, really, considering vicar's uniforms are basically long black dresses, frilly tops and a scarf," Val added with a smile.

"Well, at the moment it's not an issue," I said. "She's down south and I can keep my dressing private up here." I stubbed out the cigarette I'd been smoking and picked up my handbag. "I'm off to Dotz, are you coming?"

Chapter 12. Breakfast in Bed
Friday 1st August 1997

I still finished work at lunchtime on the Friday even though I wasn't driving home. Instead, I returned to the flat, parked in the side road and quickly changed. Half an hour later I was walking into a shop in North Manchester that sold the vagina panties I'd seen advertised. I wasn't convinced that the devices would be as effective as they claimed. Could they really allow penetrative sex? Could you really sit and pee like a woman with it? I'd be very surprised if they didn't leak.

"Well, some of our customers use period pads to catch any leakage," the assistant told me. "They say wearing the pads adds to the feeling of femininity," she added.

Possibly, I thought. But, if they gave the illusion of a female anatomy and effectively removed my penis from the equation, then that would do for me.

Looking at it, it didn't look too bad. It would certainly do a good job of hiding the penis. The photographs used in the catalogue must have been retouched to conceal where the device ended and skin started – but panties would hide the joins. The back of the device had a cut out – presumably to allow for going to the toilet and any other activity involving the arse. It was a good job the expenses credit card bill came to the flat or I could see Lucinda querying what I had spent £299 on.

I called at the supermarket on the way back to the flat to stock up for the week. I looked at some thongs. Having to have panties that controlled my penis meant I'd needed something rather more substantial. Now I could try more adventurous styles. It might also mean I could go swimming as there'd be no bulge to give me away. Perhaps it had been a good purchase after all. I put a couple of thongs and G-strings and a one-piece swimming costume in my trolley. I ensured that the cossie leg style would cover the vagina panties.

Having put the shopping away, I tried the VP on. It certainly held me in place. I put my fingers at the entrance to the vagina opening. They went in a few inches. Interesting. Even if it wouldn't work for full penetrative sex, maybe it would take a vibrator. I took out the swimming costume and tried that on. It was perfect. There was no trace of a penis; in fact, there was the hint of a camel-toe between my legs. I'd need to pad out the breasts but some 'chicken fillets' should do the trick.

Philip and I were going into the Village again this evening. I would drive over to his flat and park in the courtyard at the back. Then we'd take a taxi into town.

Putting the dress on that I'd worn for my date with Philip last Saturday I could feel my excitement building. I packed a sexy matching nightdress and negligée I'd bought during the week in my overnight bag with changes and other essentials for tomorrow and Sunday. A final check of my appearance and I was ready.

Instead of going back to Taurus, I introduced Philip to the Blue Café – then Dotz before moving on to Napoleons.

Belinda, Joan and her boyfriend and Jackie were already in there when we arrived.

"No need to ask how things went last Friday then do we?" remarked Jackie as I introduced Philip to them. "And, we noticed you weren't in here on Saturday night as you said you'd be."

"We had a meal in Taurus then went on to Via Fosse and had every intention of coming here later but decided we had something better to do," I told them, putting my arm around Philip's waist and kissing him. "Didn't we, love?" he then asked if I wanted a glass of wine and went to the bar to get our drinks.

"So come on, tell. Did you do the full deed?" Belinda demanded. I tried to give her an inscrutable look but failed miserably.

"You fucking did, didn't you? Christ, you lucky bloody cow. So, how was it?"

I closed my eyes and tried to create a dreamy look on my face.

"Shall we say I think the genie has escaped the bottle and smashed it on the way out," I said.

Just then, Philip returned with my glass of wine and we lit up cigarettes while we continued chatting to the others.

When the cheesy sequence started to play, we all joined the dance floor. As we danced, my skirt flared out from my waist showing my knickers but I wasn't worried about showing a bulge any longer. Not that it would have mattered in Naps. I loved the feel of the silky material against my skin. Once the music slowed, I was in Philip's arms, revelling in his embrace. Was this the real me? It felt so natural, so right. But I had responsibilities that couldn't be ignored.

Inevitably, the wine I'd been drinking demanded release and I excused myself and headed for the ladies. Was it possible to sit down and pee using the device? I'd wrapped a pad around my penis where it went in the sleeve to catch any leaks and was quite surprised when it seemed to work.

About two o'clock, we left the club and walked round to Village Cabs.

We had to wait nearly an hour for a taxi. But it didn't matter as we spent the time in each other's arms.

In bed, Philip examined my vagina panties and agreed to try using them for penetrative sex.

I liked the way I could position myself like a woman while we made love but had to agree with Philip that the sensations were much better the other way.

Waking up the next morning next to him, snuggling up to his back, reaching around and taking hold of his morning woody felt wonderful. I told him to stay in bed while I went to the toilet then up to the kitchen to make some coffee and toasted some bread for breakfast.

"You'd make someone a wonderful wife, you know, darling," he said as he sat up and took the tray from me. I got back under the covers with him and took a bite of the toast he'd buttered and spread with apricot jam.

We did eventually emerge from the bed. I had a shower and dressed then took the tray back up to the kitchen and washed and dried the crockery. As I was finishing, Philip came up behind me, wrapped his arms around me and nuzzled my neck. "Still playing the housewife, are you?"

I closed my eyes and leant back into his embrace. I could smell his masculine aftershave. It felt so wonderful to be held. Was this what I wanted? Would I want to live full-time as a female? It was fabulous having a weekend en-femme but what would it be like full time? Would I want to go through all of the rigamarole that Barbara, Kath and Frances at Concorde had? Hell, no! I was a guy who liked to express his feminine side – and be treated as female – but that was as far as it went. Wasn't it? It would be a real drag doing it all the time, I thought, then realised the inadvertent pun.

"What are your plans for the afternoon? I have a couple of hours work I need to do. Sorry, but I did warn you that I would."

"Yes, love, I know you did. I'm going to pop into town to pick up a few things, so that's fine."

"Your best bet is to take the bus to Piccadilly Gardens; the stop is just up the road and the buses are about every fifteen minutes, far easier than finding somewhere to park in the city centre," Philip advised.

Forty minutes later, I was wandering down Market Street window-shopping. I wanted at least two more dresses for evenings out in the Village – and who knew what else might catch my fancy. In the end, I bought three dresses, two blouses, three skirts and a pair of teal strappy sandals with three-and-half-inch heels.

The first dress was a sleeveless, boat-neck design that flared out from the waist in a red tartan material; the second also had a boat-neck but had short sleeves, a more flared skirt and was in a gorgeous teal. The last was a round-necked, long-sleeved, skater dress in a silver jersey material that felt wonderful as it swirled against my legs.

The skirts were a short blue denim skirt for round the flat; a long, multi-layered, wispy skirt with a handkerchief hemline in a light mauve and a plaid design on a grey background with pleats from the hips. I fell in love with an abstract design, long sleeve, button-through blouse in Terracotta and another navy-blue, round neck design, with a gathered yoke and short sleeves. I planned to wear the teal dress when we went out that evening with the new strappy sandals.

We decided to eat at Metz that evening; Philip had been telling me that their lamb shanks were fabulous. It was a pleasant evening so the taxi dropped us on Sackville Street and we walked down Canal Street to the bridge over the canal to the restaurant. We decided to eat on the barge rather than in the actual restaurant and ordered a bottle of Shiraz while waiting for our dinners to arrive. As we sat and drank our wine and smoked, we people-watched as the cosmopolitan crowds wandered in and out of the clubs and restaurants across the canal.

Apparently straight couples ambled past drag artists making their way from one venue to another; gay couples, of all genders, meandered by hand-in-hand or arm-in-arm, occasionally stopping to kiss. There was a mismatched, in height, couple that I knew to be a six-foot-plus transsexual with their five-foot-five wife who was staying with her partner in spite of the difficulties. There were transgender individuals wearing conventional clubbing outfits – that other women of their own age would wear – and others in leather and chains, their skirts exposing the suspenders holding up their fishnet stockings, striding along in thigh-high boots with five-inch stiletto heels, huge wigs and bizarre make-up. I recognised two or three of the other girls and waved a greeting. They waved back then moved on.

As we waited for our dinner, a woman came onto the barge with a bunch of roses in her arms. She moved from table to table trying to persuade diners to buy one for their companions. Philip signalled to her and bought one for me.

Our food arrived and was as Philip had said it would be. The meat just fell off the bone and the sauce was perfect. The waitress asked if we wanted a dessert as she cleared away our plates. I couldn't manage another mouthful, so we settled for coffee. I had a Tia Maria while Philip chose a Rémy Martin. He smoked a cigar while I stayed with my cigarettes.

As I finished my liqueur and stubbed out my cigarette, Philip drained the last of his brandy.

As we walked up the road, our arms around each other's waist, I could smell the intensely masculine aroma of Philip's cigar on his jacket; it added to my own feeling of femininity as my skirt floated around my legs, caressing them and the click, click of my heels on the pavement.

We had our usual fabulous evening in the piano bar and Napoleons before getting a cab home where we rounded off a terrific day in suitable fashion.

Sunday morning, it was my turn for breakfast in bed – where we stayed for some leisurely love-making before dressing. We then drove out to Bollington for a late lunch at the Swan with Two Nicks restaurant and a gentle stroll through the grounds of Dunham Massey to work off the calories we'd just consumed.

Then, sadly, it was time for this wonderful weekend to end. I had to return to my own flat to get ready for work. I could revel in my scented skin for another night before showering in the morning but I needed to remove every last trace of nail varnish from my finger and toe nails. There were also a few papers I needed to review ready for meetings on the Monday. It would be a very busy week as I started my annual leave on Friday.

Chapter 13. Baguettes et Croissants
Friday 8th August 1997

Leaving the office on Friday, instead of turning right for the flat, I turned left onto Princess Parkway and out past the airport. Last weekend had been incredible, but I was looking forward to seeing Olivia (and Lucinda) again. It had been a long time since I'd been away from them for three weeks. Now we'd be together for a fortnight for our annual holiday.

I put a tape into the cassette player and, once I was heading south on the M6, settled onto autopilot, cruising at between eighty and eighty-five. Traffic, as always, was heavy; though not as bad as the northbound lanes, which were solid with holidaymakers making for North Wales, the Lakes, Scotland or Blackpool. Stoke and Stafford were soon left in my wake as the BMW ate up the miles; the industrial grime of the West Midlands crowded in on both sides of the motorway and traffic slowed as we encountered the start of rush hour and became stop-start as I approached the split for the M5 and the infamous Spaghetti Junction. Then it was onto that God-awful elevated stretch hemmed in by barriers and tower blocks; past Fort Dunlop on my left. I hated this part of the M6 and couldn't wait for the long-vaunted Midland Expressway to be built; though whether I'd still be doing this journey when it opened was another question. The project would certainly have finished well before then – or I was likely to have been fired.

Clear of Birmingham, the traffic thinned and concrete buildings gave way to open fields. I relaxed, cracked open the driver's door window and lit a cigarette as my speed built up again to a little over the official speed limit. Coventry and Rugby slipped by on my right before I took the slip road for the A14 M1-A1 link; another hour or so and I'd be home.

Lucinda had booked the dogs into kennels so I was spared them jumping up my legs as I opened the door. Olivia welcomed me with a scream of 'Dad' followed by a hug and kiss. I'd missed the family and wondered if I was being an absolute idiot with Philip. Lucinda took the fish and chips I'd bought on the way for Friday's usual dinner and proceeded to serve it on plates and take it into the dining room. Olivia's friend, June, had been hanging around in the background.

"I'll be off now, Liv," she said, "see you tomorrow."

Olivia let go of me and hugged her. "Yes, it's going to be brill. Sun, sand and . . ." there was a pause.

I waited to hear what the third 'S' Olivia was going to say.

"Sea," she concluded. I shook my head.

June was coming with us on holiday to keep Olivia company; an arrangement that we'd followed since they had become best friends in junior school. She lived a few houses down the road so would bring her things round with her in the morning. We were catching the overnight ferry from Portsmouth to St Malo; then driving south through Nantes and Rennes before heading for the coast at Bordeaux and the campsite near Arcachon. Our accommodation was a two-bedroom chalet with a terrace that would be perfect for drinks while the sun set.

"How long will it take to get to Portsmouth, tomorrow?" asked Lucinda.

"About three hours, allowing for delays on the M25 past London," I told her. "If we get away about mid-day, we'll have more than enough time even if we do get held up. If we're early, we could always go and have a look around HMS Victory and have a meal before joining the ferry."

"How was your pony trekking, last weekend, Olivia?" I asked.

"It was absolutely brill. That's what I want for my birthday, a pony."

"I've told you, Olivia, we really can't afford one. It's not just the cost of buying it, you have to pay for stabling, vet's bills and feed and all sorts of other things," Lucinda told her.

"Well, what about riding lessons? It could be for both my birthday and Christmas presents," she pleaded.

I was quite certain she'd known a pony of her own would be out of the question but reducing her demand might get her what she really wanted. She probably guessed we'd have considered lessons to be too much so didn't ask for that immediately, but she knew we'd be reluctant to turn down two requests in quick succession. Clever girl.

"We'll see," I told her. That old parental stand-bye.

Being away during the week, some of the jobs I used to do in the lighter evenings, like mowing the lawns, keeping the borders tidy and washing the cars, now had to be crammed into my weekends. I'd been thinking of hiring someone to take over that work. Olivia already helped her mum around the house but if she was happy to take that on, the budget could go to riding lessons instead.

I discussed the idea with Lucinda later. We decided that if Olivia did the extra tasks, we'd agree to fortnightly lessons. Later, when she was able to earn money from a part-time job, we'd match what she earned towards lessons.

In bed, I reached for Lucinda. I'd learned, with Philip, some of what it felt like to have someone make love to you as a female – but how could I apply those lessons without Lucinda wondering why I'd suddenly changed my technique? How could I even raise the subject? I didn't have an answer but it saddened me that sex with Philip was so much more exciting than with Lucinda.

The next morning, after breakfast, I took the car to the garage, filled up and checked the tyres, oil, water and washer fluid. When I returned home, June had arrived with her luggage.

The drive down to Portsmouth was uneventful, so we did have time for a bit of sightseeing and dinner before joining the queue for the ferry.

We'd booked a four-berth cabin as this was safer than the girls being in a separate cabin. I went on deck while Lucinda, Olivia and June got ready for bed and had a cigarette, only my second that day – the first while I was out getting the car filled up. Lucinda sent me a text when they were all decent again and I returned to the cabin, took my things into the bathroom and showered and changed. I climbed into my bunk, wished everyone good-night and switched off the light.

Next morning, I dressed first then went on deck for a smoke while the others sorted themselves out. We had breakfast in the cafeteria before the ship docked in St Malo and it was time to return to the car.

We broke the journey every couple of hours as we made our way south. By mid-afternoon, we were on the outskirts of Bordeaux and on our final leg to the holiday park. Having checked in, we were given directions to our chalet. Lucinda and I had a compact bedroom with a double bed while the two girls' room had bunk beds. We left it to them to decide who was having which. Within half an hour, we'd unloaded the car and stowed everything and the girls had changed into swimming costumes under T-shirts and shorts and headed for the pool. Lucinda wanted to get a few essentials such as milk and some fruit from the mini-market so she walked with them towards the centre. Having done all the driving, I thought I'd earned a break and wandered off towards the beach where I could have a sneaky cigarette before returning to the chalet for a shower.

I was sitting on the terrace, drinking a glass of wine, when Lucinda arrived back with her shopping.

"Fancy a glass?" I asked, showing her the bottle.

"Mmm, yes, please," she answered, picking up the spare glass I'd put on the table for her and holding it out to me. She sank into the seat next to me, tilted her sunhat down to shade her eyes and sighed.

"This is really lovely. I had a quick look at the menu for the restaurant. I've booked a table for eight-thirty. I've told the girls to be back at seven-thirty."

Eating out had always been the plan, rather than cooking on our first evening. I looked at my watch, it was just after six-fifteen.

"That gives us just over an hour," I remarked.

"For what?" Lucinda asked.

I gestured my head towards the chalet and raised my eyebrows.

"At this time? When the girls could come back? Don't be obscene. Really!"

I hadn't honestly expected any other response. Lucinda seemed to have become increasingly strait-laced since she started to attend a church which had links to an evangelical Southern Baptist group. These days, if we did have sex, it was routine. If I tried to adopt anything other than a basic missionary position, Lucinda would roll over on her back. When I recently made a move to give her oral, she was horrified.

"What are you doing?" she'd demanded.

When I'd been with Philip, I wondered if it was my fault our love-making had become so stale. I wasn't saying none of it was my fault, but Lucinda certainly didn't help.

I picked up the book I'd been reading and settled down to 'The Perfect Storm' – the story of a fishing boat caught when three storm fronts collided to form huge waves and immense winds off Newfoundland. It occurred to me that my transvestism, the relationship with Philip and my marriage might also combine to create a perfect storm; and, if they did, then my chances of survival wouldn't be great. I must be mad to risk everything as I did.

The sun was low in the sky and a gentle breeze was dissipating the heat of the day as we walked over to the restaurant; whispers of smoke from other holidaymakers' barbecues and the aroma of their dinners mingled with the scent of the pine woods surrounding the site. In the restaurant, we were being shown to our table when a girl grabbed Olivia's arm.

"Bonsoir, Olivia, bonsoir, June,"

"Oh, hi, Collette, hi Odette, this is my mum and dad. Mum and Dad, we met Collette and Odette at the pool this afternoon."

The adults sitting at the table stood up; two boys with them remained seated.

"I am Giselle, mother to these children and this is my husband, Claude. The boys are Michel and Armand," announced the woman. Turning to the boys she cont nued "Michel, Armand, levez-vous et dites bonsoir."

Claude held out his hand and we shcok.

"I'm Chris and this is my wife, Lucinda. Olivia is our daughter and June is her best friend, keeping her company on holiday. Very nice to meet you. Please don't let us interrupt your dinner though," I said.

"We will be moving into the salon after eating, perhaps you would like to join us for a drink after your meal?" Giselle suggested.

"That would be lovely," Lucinda agreed as the maître de coughed to remind us he was waiting to show us to our table.

Our table was next to a window giving a view of the sun setting over the trees, casting a glorious red glow promising a beautiful tomorrow.

"Such a pleasant family," Lucinda commented as we strolled back to our chalet three hours later. "So nice that you've already made friends here, girls. I hope you're going to use the opportunity to practice your French and not just let them speak English."

"Oui, Maman," said Olivia, with a giggle.

"Oui, Tante Lucinda," echoed June.

In the morning, Olivia and June volunteered to go to the boulangerie for fresh flaky croissants for breakfast and crispy baguettes for lunch. By the time they returned, however, both ends of one of the baguettes had disappeared.

The holiday fled past in days spent n the water park at the campsite, at the beach just three miles away or on excursions.

We particularly liked the lake at Biscarosse. The water was only thigh deep for about fifty metres out from the shore before the bottom dropped away almost vertically. The shallow areas were ideal for learning to windsurf. If you fell off, it was easy to climb back on the board. Both Olivia and June soon got the hang of standing with feet apart and pulling the sail up out of the water, gripping the boom and adjusting the sails to glide across the water. It wasn't long before they were shuffling around the front of the sail to tack and sailing off in a new direction. Inevitably there were occasional screams from them as manoeuvres went wrong and they fell off the boards. I entered a competition one afternoon and was satisfied coming fifth out of twelve competitors.

Lucinda chose to lie on the beach most of the time; looking after our belongings. She tutted at some of the other women who were sunbathing topless. I couldn't help admiring their breasts – not the usual male ogling but because I was imagining what it would be like to have breasts of my own and the clothes I could then wear.

Then I looked at Olivia and a shiver went down my spine at the thought of my secret being found out and the devastation that would cause. I really did have to deal with those urges.

Not far from the lake, was the Dune de Pilat, the biggest sand dune in Europe. As the sun started to drop towards the horizon and the midday heat started to fade, we parked the car near the base and climbed the steps to the summit. The seaward side was busy with parascenders flying along, supported by the updraft from the winds striking the 110 metres high barrier and the rising air, warmed as the sun's rays heated the white sand. We sat and watched the sun set over the ocean; its colour changing to a deep orange as it dipped below the horizon.

Eventually, it was time for us to pack the car for the drive back to St Malo and our ferry home.

We arrived back on August Bank holiday weekend. Fortunately, the traffic, as we took the M3 towards London, tended to be heading to the coast so we had a relatively easy drive home on the Sunday. Monday was a bank holiday so I was off work and was going to catch up with cutting the grass when Olivia shouted.

"Dad, you said I could do that and you'd put the money to riding lessons." I was happy to let her take it over having made sure that she understood the importance of keeping the power lead away from the blades. I heard the phone ringing while I was in the garden. Lucinda answered it.

She came nto the garden a few minutes later.

"That was Mum. She asked if I could take Olivia down to see them again for the autumn half-term holiday. Would you mind? We'd be away for two weekends again."

I told her that would be fine with me. Then I raised a suggestion I'd been considering.

"I'm expecting there to be a lot to catch up on this week at work, especially as it's only four days. I was thinking about staying in Manchester next weekend to clear the backlog. How would you feel about that?"

I knew that she could hardly object as, as far as she was aware, I'd accepted her being away for two weekends at the beginning of the month and had just agreed to another two in October.

Chapter 14. TV Dinners
Tuesday 26th August 1997

As expected, there was a pile of work waiting for me when I got to the office after the holiday. I made myself a mug of coffee and started to plough through the paperwork and emails and sorted everything into 'immediate', 'urgent' and 'can wait' piles. Fortunately, no major problems had cropped up while I'd been away. I was, nevertheless, very happy to have dealt with nearly all of the first two categories by the end of the day. Everything else could wait until tomorrow. Logging off my computer, I tidied my desk then pushed my chair away from the desk, leaned back and stared out of the window.

I watched as an aircraft made its approach to the airport. There had been a time when I could identify nearly all commercial and military aircraft but, these days, most airliners seemed to have their two or four engines slung under the wings and differentiating between one of the Boeing 737 variants and several Airbus models was now beyond me. Now, I had other interests – and challenges.

Back at the flat, I put the ready meal I would have that evening to one side and put away the rest of the groceries I'd picked up at the supermarket. I then phoned home for a quick chat with Olivia and Lucinda.

As I was getting ready to shower, I heard the theme from Monty Python sounding from Christine's mobile phone. It was Philip. A shiver of anticipation ran down my spine at the thought of seeing him again.

"Hi, babe, how was the holiday? Are you coming over this evening?"

I hadn't been sure what time I'd finish work – so we'd left it open.

"Yes, love, I was just about to give you a call to confirm. I'm going to get a shower and change, have a bite to eat then come over."

"You don't need to change, you know. You can come over as you are – it doesn't matter to me."

It might not matter to Philip but it did to me.

"Sorry, darling – but I have to be Christine with you. Don't worry, it won't take me too long to get ready. I'll be with you by nine."

As I disconnected the call, I reflected that Philip's "OK, see you when you get here," sounded unenthusiastic. Maybe we needed to talk this through when I got there.

After my shower, I put on my undies and kimono to eat my dinner. It amused me that the manufacturers described the meals as TV dinners.

Back in the bedroom, I smoked a cigarette while I did my make-up and finished dressing. A spritz of perfume and I was ready to leave.

The familiar drive to Philip's didn't take long and I was soon parking outside his house. He must have been watching for me as the front door opened as I reached it.

As he closed the door behind us, I turned to face him and wrapped my arms around his neck; he pulled me close, gripping my bum and pressing his crotch against me. Our lips met and I felt his tongue probing hungrily – I responded eagerly. We eventually came up for air.

"Did you miss me then?" he asked with a twinkle in his eye.

I pressed against him. "What do you think?" I asked.

"Show me," he said, taking my hand and starting up the stairs.

Scented candles lit the bedroom and a bottle of Champagne was chilling in an ice bucket next to two glasses.

Afterwards, as we sat drinking the fizz and smoking, Philip turned to me.

"I want you to move in with me. I want to fall asleep with my arms around you and wake up next to you every morning."

I kissed him gently on his lips then looked him in the eyes.

"That would be fabulous but I can't. You know I can't. I have to be at work by half eight."

"Why is that a problem? It's only another ten minutes."

"If I went straight there, that's true – but I'd need to dress and make-up here, go home, get changed then drive to the office."

"But you don't need to dress as female. Look, I know when we first got together, I wasn't ready to admit I was gay. I needed someone who looked female but was actually male. I'm over that now and ready to move on and have a full-time boyfriend."

I sat there, trying to work out how to respond.

"Maybe I don't need to appear female for you, Philip, but I do for me. I don't see myself as gay. Maybe that's just me being in denial. When I'm dressed, Christine takes over and that's who I become." I took a drag on my cigarette. "As Christine, I love having a guy treat me as female and behaving as one. As a guy, I have no interest in sex with another man. I'm sorry, but there it is."

Philip lay back in the bed staring into space. Was this going to be the end of our relationship?

He sighed.

"I see. Trouble is, Chris, you dressing as female makes me feel I'm not being true to my sexuality. It's as though I'm still not totally accepting that I'm gay by having sex with someone presenting as female. Some of my other gay friends are also questioning if I'm gay enough for some of the venues in the Gay Village."

I lit another cigarette and took a deep drag on it to give me time to think about my response.

"So, are you saying you want to stop seeing me?"

He took my hand in his. "No, babe. I love being with you. You make me laugh, we share so many interests and you're fabulous in bed. But I want us to be boyfriends, not boy and girl. There are places I'd like to go with you in the Village that don't admit women or trannies."

Could I do it? Could I go out with Philip as male?

Did I want to do it?

As Christine, I segregated my cross-dressing and affair with Philip from my life as Lucinda's husband and Olivia's father. That was important to me. Maybe it was a pretence but it was one I could live with. If I went out with Philip as Christopher, the boundaries would disappear.

I turned on my side to face Philip. "I'm sorry, but I can't do it. I can't be with you as a guy. I have to keep my male and female sides separate. If that means it's over between us, I'll be very sad. What we've had has been fabulous. But, if you've moved on and need something different, I understand. I'm sorry I can't give you what you want."

He just lay there; staring at the ceiling. I wondered what he was thinking. I guessed he was deciding what was more important to him. Would he decide he could accept me dressing as female and not being able to take me to some clubs – but enjoying the benefits of having me around? Or would he decide having a full-time live-in boyfriend was more important to him? Did he have someone in mind in case I turned him down? I didn't think so. If that had been true, surely he wouldn't be thinking about what to do. Would he?

I got my answer a few moments later.

He rolled on top of me and pressed his lips onto mine forcing his tongue into my mouth. He lifted his head and shook it.

"You win. I want you. So, if that means as female then that's how it has to be."

He squatted back on his ankles, lifted my legs over his shoulders, rolled a condom onto his stiff penis and penetrated.

As I drove home, I wondered how long Philip would accept me as Chris. I was quite certain making love after our discussion had been a reprieve rather than a capitulation. Sooner or later, I knew he would move on. Well, when that did happen, I could hardly complain.

My thoughts were interrupted as the lights at a pedestrian crossing ahead changed to amber so I slowed and stopped. At the side of me, a couple of teenagers ambled towards the crossing. They glanced into the car and looked straight at me. Had they clocked me? I felt an icy chill up my spine and reached to check that I'd locked the passenger door. As my fingers touched the button, the door was wrenched open. Shit, I hadn't locked it before driving off earlier.

A hand grabbed my handbag and the two youths ran down a side street blocked by bollards, preventing me from following them in the car even if I'd been inclined to do so. Not that I was tempted at all. I didn't want to risk a stabbing.

I was annoyed with myself for not having stowed the bag more securely and for failing to lock the doors when I'd left Philip's. The keys to the flat were with the car's, in the ignition. As for the handbag, it was just one I'd bought in Debenhams. The purse in it probably contained about thirty pounds. Apart from that, there was some make-up and Christine's inexpensive mobile phone. Certainly not worth worrying about — or reporting to the police and having to answer awkward questions.

Most of the cars behind me pulled out to pass as I sat there. One other driver got out of his car and approached me.

"Are you OK love?" he asked.

"I'm fine, thanks," I told him.

"Not a good idea driving through this area without locking your doors. Mind you they then smash the windows," he told me. "Would you like me to close your passenger door?"

I couldn't reach it from the driver's seat and didn't want to get out of the car to do it myself so I nodded my head. "Yes, please. Thanks."

I waved my thanks as I pulled away. I lit a cigarette and opened the window slightly to draw out the smoke as I exhaled.

It had been a narrow escape. I knew car-jacking was a problem and I'd been lucky that they'd only wanted my handbag. If they'd tried to take the car, I might well have been hurt. God, the complications that would have been caused if the police had beccme involved — not to mention a possible trip to A&E and getting back into the flat without the keys.

Chapter 15. Baked Potatoes
Friday 31st October 1997

Over the next few months, I got into a routine of commuting straight to the Manchester office early on a Monday morning. The rest of the week, I'd get into the office around eight. I'd work through to about six then drive to the flat – calling at a local supermarket on the way if I needed any supplies.

Most evenings, I'd phone home and chat to Olivia and Lucinda about their days before having a shower and dressing. Monday evenings, after dinner and washing up, I'd take out the laptop, and catch up on paperwork. Wednesday evenings was Concord group – so I'd change as soon as I got back to the flat then drive to the Village and have a meal at the Blue Café before walking round to the group; getting there about 8.30.

Lucinda and Olivia had been away at Lucinda's parents the previous two weekends and I'd spent them with Philip. He still dropped hints about me not needing to dress for him and how that would let me stay over more often. I sensed increasing irritation over my stance, but it was how I felt and that was an end to it.

On Fridays, after a meeting with the project team, I'd have a conference call with Head Office then drive home.

This Saturday, there was a firework display in our village, held on the sports field next to the village hall. The cost was met by an annual quiz and other fundraising events. As we entered the field through the gate, we greeted some of our neighbours then joined the queue for baked potatoes.

We stood next to the rope separating the spectators from the bonfire and firework display. Flames started to flicker from the bottom of the pile of timber, boxes and other assorted material that had been collected over the last couple of weeks. I had no doubt that if we'd been in a large town or city, rival gangs would have set fire to it before the big night. Thankfully, our village was relatively crime-free. Within minutes, the fire had grown and was licking at the feet of the Guy at the top of the bonfire. Sparks were carried away on the breeze; shooting stars against the black sky.

June's family, the Edwards, found us standing by the rope, finishing our baked potatoes; the two girls greeted each other as though they'd been separated for weeks instead of less than three hours. Douglas, June's father, gave the two girls sparklers and lit them; they stepped away from us waving their arms in circles and giggling. June's mother, Maureen, and Lucinda saw another friend of theirs so wandered off for a chat.

"So, Chris, how's the project going in Manchester?" Douglas enquired.

"Fine, thanks, Dougie. Hectic, but we're pretty much on schedule," I answered.

"Time enough for a bit of fun though, I'll bet. I heard you'd stayed up there a couple of weekends. Plenty of crumpet in the clubs, I dare say. Have you been to the Hacienda? Or are you more interested in the footie?"

"I wouldn't even know where the Hacienda is, not really my scene – never has been. I'm probably too old for it these days, in any case, probably full of teenagers and twenty-somethings. And I've no interest at all in football, rugby's my sport if anything."

"Doesn't that just about get you lynched in Manchester, surely that's bordering on heresy?"

I shrugged my shoulders, "True, so I keep quiet about it."

"Sounds like a wasted opportunity, if you ask me. Footloose and fancy-free a hundred and fifty miles from home? Come on, what did you really do?"

I tapped the side of my nose and looked around furtively. "Can you keep a secret?" I whispered.

"Absolutely," he replied, conspiratorially.

"So can I," I said laughing. "If you must know, I spent most of one day doing the laundry then went out for a meal on my own at a curry house in Rusholme, it's known as Curry Mile. Another day, I visited the Museum of Science and Industry. Exciting enough for you?"

"You disappoint me, Chris," he said shaking his head.

I suspected for all his comments, that if he had been on his own in Manchester, his time would have been spent as I'd described. Or would it? Maybe he had his secrets too. We really don't ever know other people; he certainly didn't know me. At least, I hoped he didn't.

Our conversation was cut short by the first rocket shooting into the sky and exploding to a chorus of oohs and aahs. The display alternated between ground level and overhead. As the bonfire continued to burn itself out, the tall flames wafting this way and that in the wind giving way to an orange glow. The heat it had been providing diminished and the wind started to give the promise of snow as it bit into any exposed skin. Once the last of the fireworks had died, we turned for home, walking along with the Edwards family until we reached our house where we said our goodnights.

"Anyone for cocoa?" Lucinda asked.

Both Olivia and I accepted the offer leaving her to prepare it while we went into the lounge. The dogs had been left in the hall, insulated as far as possible from any firework noise. We were far enough from the display for the explosions to be subdued – and most of the residents abided by an unwritten agreement not to have private displays that included 'bangs'.

"Come on, Max, come on Maya. Out you go and do your business," Olivia instructed the dogs as she opened the back door. "The nasty bangs have finished. But be quick."

I went through to the lounge and put another log on the fire. That was one thing I missed in the flat. There is nothing like the smell of burning logs and the visual warmth of a fire. We'd had the fireplace rebuilt when we'd moved in. In place of a boring brick surround, we had buff Cotswold stone with a small alcove on each side for ornaments; a grey granite hearth and a dark teak mantlepiece. Either side of the chimney breast were tall G-plan units. The three-piece suite and the coffee table were also G-plan. It was, perhaps, firmly 70s but it was all well-built and solid, so reflected the family – or, at least, the impression we created. 'Christine' rather broke from that image.

"Why don't you come to Church anymore?" Lucinda asked the next morning as she pulled on her gloves and adjusted her hat. "It doesn't set a good example for Olivia, you know. She keeps asking why she has to go when you don't."

I could have said that I thought the minister was bigoted and hypocritical and that I really didn't want to hear his evangelical rants about the absolute truth of the Bible. I totally sympathised with Olivia. I didn't see why she should be forced to attend.

I'd been brought up in the Church of England but I'd started to question religion when I faced the church's stance on gay and transgender people. At first, I'd tried to find explanations for St Paul's epistles condemning homosexuality and verses describing cross-dressing as an abomination. Eventually, instead of considering them misinterpretations, I came to question the authority of the Bible as a whole.

For me it boiled down to 'for the Bible to be the indisputable word of God, it had to be totally accurate. If any part of it was questionable, then the entirety was questionable.'

In any case, why would a loving God create beings that were attracted to others of the same gender – then condemn them for acting on those feelings? Or create others with the body of one sex but the identity of another? Why? Why would a creator find that an abomination? If God didn't make mistakes, why did they create evil – or allow it to be created if they were omnipotent? Why shouldn't you wear garments of mixed fibres? Why should an individual being illegitimate mean their great-grandchildren were sinful?

And why did the God of the Abrahamic religions create other religions with different Gods that survived for thousands of years before Judaism, Christianity and Islam were founded? Why didn't that God just create one religion, from the start, all around the world?

I could understand religions as mystical explanations for things that early communities didn't understand and some of their rules as guidance for civilised behaviour. But I didn't want to be lectured by someone I despised.

Knowing I wasn't going to debate the issue with her, Lucinda turned away.

"Come on Olivia, or we'll be late."

Olivia's eyes pleaded with me to rescue her – but there was no point in trying to argue with Lucinda.

Chapter 16. Beans on Toast
Monday 3rd November 1997

Monday evening, I saw a message from Philip on my 'Christine' phone. It read 'Sorry, can't see you this week.' There were no 'P' or 'x's – our usual sign-offs. Strange. I rang him but it went to voice mail so I left a message and hung up, pulled out my laptop and started on some paperwork..

He hadn't returned my call by Wednesday so I phoned again and it still went through to voice-mail. I was getting a bit concerned. As I got ready to go out, I decided to call at his house on my way into the Village. The house was in darkness and there was no reply to the bell so I got back in the car and drove off. Maybe he was away this week; it would have been good to have had an explanation rather than the terse message he'd sent – but, perhaps, there'd been an emergency of some sort. I realised I knew little about his family. Well, time would tell.

As usual, I parked up on Bloom Street. It was convenient for the Blue Café, where I'd have my dinner and for Napoleons later in the evening – and not that far down the road to the venue for the support group. As I turned the corner by Napoleons, I thought I saw Philip going into the Rembrandt with two other guys. I couldn't be totally positive; it was raining and the nearest streetlight was across the road from him. I could have followed him in but the Rem wasn't particularly trans friendly. If it had been Philip, and he was with other friends, I wasn't sure he'd welcome me intruding. In any case, he was perfectly entitled to go out with whoever he wanted. We weren't connected at the hips after all.

After dinner, I strolled down to the Rem and turned onto Canal Street. I tried to spot Philip through the windows but, if he was in there, I didn't see him. I made my way down to Hollywood Showbar where I joined some friends for a few drinks before we headed to Napoleons for a bit of a boogie. It was a great night out – the last for a few days for Christine.

Friday's journey home was an absolute nightmare. A storm had blown in from the Atlantic and was pounding the country. Torrential rain reduced visibility to less than fifty yards at times even when not being hit by the spray from lorries. Gusts were making it difficult for those HGVs that managed to stay upright, to keep in their lanes and I was nearly side-swiped several times. There were three separate tailbacks for accidents between Walsall and Coventry; each delaying me for fifteen to twenty minutes.

With my reduced speed, instead of arriving home by five-thirty (after calling for fish and chips), it was gone nine. The chippy had closed and I was totally shattered. I'd called Lucinda on my hands-free phone and she and Olivia had eaten earlier. She rustled up some beans on toast for me – I was so tired; I couldn't face anything more substantial.

After dinner, I poured a stiff measure of Glenfiddich whisky, a Christmas present from the in-laws, took it into the lounge and slumped into a chair. I stared at the flames licking around the logs on the fire – sparks flying up the chimney as the oil in the hunks of pine exploded giving off a fabulous, relaxing scent.

Olivia sat next to me, put her arms around my neck and kissed me. I put my arm around her and held her close.

"I was so worried about you, Daddy."

"Well, I'm here now and I'm fine."

"Yes, but if the weather is that bad in future, wouldn't it make more sense to stay in Manchester? Winter's coming and much as we want to see you at weekends, Chris, we'd rather miss you for a weekend than have you hurt," Lucinda pointed out.

By Monday morning, the storm had passed but the devastation it had left was evident as I drove north. There were buildings on industrial estates without roofs, trees down in fields next to the motorway and deep grooves in verges where vehicles had been blown off the carriageways. Rivers visible from the motorway were in full flood and had burst their banks in places. It wasn't as bad as the storm of 1987 which had left swathes of woodland flattened but still bad enough. As the saying goes,

'It's an ill wind that blows nobody any good," and this one had given me another excuse for weekends in Manchester.

I still hadn't heard back from Philip. Were we meeting up this week or not? After changing that evening, I rang him and, to my amazement, he picked up.

"Ah. Hi Chris. I've been meaning to give you a call."

I could tell from his tone that I wasn't going to like what he was about to tell me.

"The thing is, there's no easy way to say this, but I think we should stop seeing each other."

I guess I'd known this was coming since that text last week.

"I see; actually, no I don't. Unless you're seeing someone else. Is that it?"

There was a pause.

"Yes, there is. Look, we had fun. Didn't we? But I'm sorry I wanted more than you could give me. It was great at the start but occasional weekends and Tuesdays and Thursday evenings weren't enough. I wanted someone full-time. And, now I think I've found him."

There didn't seem to be anything else to say so I ended the call.

I lit a cigarette and sat back in my chair.

I didn't blame Philip for wanting more than I could give him. It wasn't that we'd made declarations of undying love. Realistically, the attraction had been lust. I'd enjoyed the way he'd treated me as female but I didn't love him. I'd miss the sex, obviously.

Wednesday evening at Concorde, I saw the usual gang at a table and waved to them while I ordered a drink. Picking up my glass, I joined them and said hello. Belinda wouldn't meet my eyes for some reason.

"Something wrong?" I asked.

"Just tell her," Jackie said.

"Tell me what?" I demanded.

"I was in Mantos on Saturday evening and saw Philip in there with a young guy," Belinda told me.

"Yeah, I spoke to him on Monday and he said he was with someone else now."

"Shit, I'm sorry to hear that; well, his loss," Belinda said.

"He wanted more than I could give," I said with a shrug. I lit a cigarette and took a sip of my wine. "He wanted me to move in with him and that wasn't possible. I didn't want a gay relationship."

"I did wonder if this would happen," Michelle remarked. "Well, plenty more fish in the sea as they say."

Chapter 17. Lamb Shank
5th December 1997

Some of the other local girls had organised a 'Face-to-Face' gathering in Manchester for members of an online trans forum. I'd told Lucinda that I needed to stay in Manchester for the weekend. She hadn't even asked why, though I did have an excuse prepared. The organisers of the get-together had asked local members if they could offer accommodation for out-of-town visitors. I'd been reluctant to help as I wanted to keep my flat discreet – not even Philip had been there.

But Michaela phoned me in a panic on the Friday morning as I was about to leave for work.

"Leanne has been rushed into hospital with appendicitis and we desperately need a bed for Sara, who was stopping with her. She's already on her way down from Inverness, arriving at Piccadilly station about three-thirty. Is there any way you can help out?"

I'd exchanged a few messages with Sara on the forum and we had similar opinions. She'd transitioned and was living full-time as female. I'd seen photographs of her and she was unlikely to attract unwanted attention at the flat.

"OK, Michaela, yes. I can put her up. I'll meet her at Piccadilly station – have you got her mobile number?"

"Thank God for that. I really didn't want to have to tell her to turn around at Edinburgh or that she'd have to stump up for a hotel with City at home to Wolves."

I entered Sara's number into my phone – then pressed 'call'.

"Hi Sara, it's Christine in Manchester. Michaela's asked me to give you a call. I'll be putting you up instead of Leanne. I'm afraid all I can offer is a sofa – but it should be comfortable enough."

"That's fine. I think that's all Leanne had in any case. And thanks a million. I'd hate to miss the get-together. Your drinks are on me this weekend, of course."

"No need for that. Look, text me when the train gets to Bolton. That gives me time to get to Piccadilly station. I'll be in a dark blue BMW 318 the number ends 126P."

"OK, will do. I'm wearing a beige raincoat over jumper and jeans tucked into brown suede knee-length boots."

I finished work as usual for a Friday about lunchtime and returned to the flat. I changed into a skirt and casual top before having a quick tidy round.

Just after three, the text from Sara arrived and I set off for the station. She was waiting for me near the taxi queue and waved when she saw my car. Having pulled into a pick-up bay, I got out and opened the boot for her to put her case in.

"It's really good of you to put me up. You know, you're the first other trans individual I've ever met in person."

"Well, you'll be meeting quite a few others this weekend."

"Any idea how many are coming to the face-to-face?"

"Not really. I think there are about twenty of us booked for the dinner at Metz tomorrow evening – but there may be others who are meeting up later and some this evening who can't make tomorrow."

I decided to drive through the Village to show Sara where we would be this evening.

"That's Canal Street," I told her as we crossed the bridge on Sackville Street. "Metz, where we're having the dinner tomorrow is just down there." I then pointed out the Blue Café, Dotz, Napoleons and Paddy's Goose. "We'll be in all of them tonight. I'd planned to have dinner in the Blue Café before meeting the others in Paddy's Goose about nine. Are you OK with that?"

"Absolutely," she replied. "What's the dress code for this evening?"

"Whatever you want. Tomorrow's kind of the gala evening so I'm planning to dress up for that. This evening, I'm going more for a clubby look. I don't really do ultra-short skirts though others will."

Back at the flat, Sara produced a bottle of Cava.

"Can we put this in the fridge for later?" she asked. "It's a bit too warm to drink right now after ten hours travelling."

I took it from her and swopped it for one in the fridge.

"In the best Blue Peter tradition, I just happen to have a bottle I put to chill earlier," I told her.

I poured a couple of glasses and we took them into the lounge.

Sara looked at the sofa and pressed down on the seat. "This looks perfect. Thanks again."

As we drank our wine and smoked, I outlined the plan for the evening. After taking turns to shower and use the dressing table mirror to do our make-up, Sara showed me the dress she planned to wear.

"What do you think?" she asked, holding a scarlet, mid-thigh length dress against her body. "It's the first time I've ever been out in the evening as myself. Not too much, is it?"

"Not at all, it looks fabulous, let's see it on you," I told her.

Having been on hormones for a while, she had the cleavage to show off and the dress did so perfectly. I wished I could do the same – but I had to wear outfits that hid my false breasts. Tonight, I was wearing a midnight blue, boat-necked, short-sleeved blouse over a flared black calf-length skirt.

The taxi picked us up and took us into the Village, dropping us on Sackville Street opposite the Blue Café. Sara insisted on paying the driver.

"It's the least I can do for your hospitality."

We crossed over the road and I held the door open for her to enter.

Jamie, the waiter, showed us to a table and handed us menus.

"The special for tonight is Chicken Jambalaya, ladies. Can I get you drinks while you decide what you want?" he asked.

After dinner, we walked round to Paddy's Goose, bought drinks at the bar and joined the group that was already ensconced in 'Tranny Corner'. I knew several but there were a number of others from around the country here for the 'face-to-face' that I'd only ever chatted to online. Sara hadn't met anyone before. It wasn't long, however, before she was part of the conversation as though she'd known them for years.

The group eventually split up. Some going to the New Union, others to New York, New York while a few of us went to Dotz Piano Bar. We'd all meet up again in Napoleons in a couple of hours for a dance.

We got back to the flat sometime after two am. Sara's bottle of Cava was nicely chilled by then so we took it into the lounge, kicked off our shoes and slumped onto the sofa.

"Well, what did you think of that?" I asked.

"Incredible. I can't remember having so much fun. I might have to move down here," she replied.

After chatting for another half hour or so, I showed Sara the bedding for her and said I was going to bed myself. She stood up and gave me a hug.

"Thanks very much. I really appreciate this."

We didn't have breakfast at the flat the next morning as a lot of us were meeting at Paddy's Goose for brunch. It was a bit strange as some of them had reverted to male role and trying to associate the female names of the night before with the new appearances wasn't easy. Sara was wearing a simple short-sleeved blouse over jeans and boots with a leather jacket over the top. I was in a jumper and skirt. I remembered that someone had said you could always tell the crossdressers from the transsexuals and cisgendered women in the Village. The cross-dressers wore skirts or dresses, the cis-women wore trousers and the transsexuals showed off their boobs. It wasn't politically correct but it was often accurate.

After brunch, lots of the girls went off to do some shopping or, in a couple of cases, get their ears pierced. We'd all meet up again for the dinner in Metz.

Sara and I decided to go back to the flat, so we returned to the car. We spent the afternoon just chatting, drinking coffee and smoking. Sara told me about her transition; how she'd spent years identifying as a cross-dresser before deciding she needed to transition fully, how that decision had cost her job, her family and her home, and how she'd struggled to get treatment on the NHS but had final y done so. She was now waiting for surgery which she hoped to get sometime the following year.

"Was it worth it, then?" I asked.

"There wasn't really any alternative. It was that or top myself. It was hard losing contact with the kids but I just hope they'll learn to accept me as I am sometime in the future. I hope you never have to face the same decision."

"I don't plan to. I'm quite happy cross-dressing but remaining male at my core."

"Yeah. I thought the same for a long time. But, don't worry, it's by no means inevitable."

It certainly gave me something to think about. But not tonight. This evening, we had the dinner to look forward to.

The tax dropped us off at the back entrance of Metz and we made our way through the buzzing restaurant to the table that had been reserved for the dinner. Michaela and the visitors stopping at her flat in Salford had already arrived; as had several other local girls and some I recognised from the previous evening.

Nearly everyone had dressed up for the night. I'd chosen a cerise calf-length A-line dress with a boat neckline which I'd accessorised with ruby and gold drop earrings and matching necklace and bracelet. Sara looked stunning in an emerald version of the dress she'd worn the night before.

"I couldn't make up my mind between the two," she explained, "so I bought both."

The restaurant had provided free bottles of wine for the table and the waiters soon filled our glasses then returned to serve the meals we'd ordered in advance. I'd chosen the lamb shanks served in a fabulous sauce. It was my go-to dish whenever I ate at Metz. I looked up and down the table. Nearly everyone was chatting away like lifelong friends – yet I knew that this weekend was the first time that many of the group had ever met other trans people. Some had never even been out in public dressed. We were fortunate, in Manchester, to have one of the best scenes in the world on our doorstep. It was ironic that the Village had been created by a Chief Police Officer wanting to keep all the undesirables in one location. I drank a silent toast to him!

As we walked up Canal Street, on our way round to Dotz after dinner, a group of football supporters were crossing the Sackville Street bridge over the canal. They stared and pointed at us.

"Are you lot men or women?" one called out.

Wendy, who was about six feet tall and well-built was at the front of our group with Michaela and replied.

"More of a man than you'll ever be. More of a woman than you'll ever have."

I watched as the hecklers, taken aback by the response, seemed to drag their knuckles along the ground as they walked away.

Chapter 18. Christmas Pudding
19th December 1997

The Friday before Christmas, I finished work for two weeks. I'd managed to do my Christmas shopping in Manchester during the week and had bought Lucinda a gorgeous silver necklace with a Tanzanite pendant and matching drop earrings. I'd been very tempted to keep them for myself – or buy two sets. Lucinda had bought Olivia's present of riding boots, show jacket and jodhpurs. Goodness knows what the family had bought me – or what Lucinda and Olivia had bought for the dogs. I sometimes felt that more thought went into their gifts than mine. We were spending the holiday with Lucinda's parents in Hastings. We'd drive down on the Tuesday to try and avoid the mass exodus from London on Christmas Eve and the inevitable chaos it would cause on the M25.

I'd made reasonable time getting home and we'd just finished our usual Friday night fish and chips when we heard the sound of carol singers. Opening the door, we could see the local Round Table's traditional charity sleigh with Santa – or, to be more accurate, a trailer decorated as a sleigh towed behind a four-by-four. It slowly made its way along the road with the singers walking alongside backed by a loudspeaker system in the vehicle. Santa, played by Dougie, and his elves, including Olivia's friend June, visited every house, holding buckets for donations. Not wanting to lose face, I dropped a fiver into the bucket that Dougie held out for me.

Saturday evening, we met up again with Dougie, Maureen and June and the six of us went out for a meal at the Plough restaurant on the High Street in the village. There was a blustery wind blowing but no indication that it would be a white Christmas. The clouds were scudding across the sky but, fortunately, the threatened rain held off. Being able to walk to the restaurant meant we didn't have to worry about drink driving but, even so, we limited ourselves to a couple of bottles between us – plus liqueurs with our coffees.

Dougie teased me over getting up to mischief in Manchester – much as he'd done on bonfire night. Olivia defended me against accusations that I spent all my time in discos.

"Dad wouldn't do that, Uncle Dougie," she'd said.

"Of course, he wouldn't," Lucinda confirmed. "He's far too old for that."

"Hang on a minute," I protested. "I'm not past it yet."

"Ah," said Dougie. "So, you do hit the bright lights. I knew it."

I stopped digging the hole I was getting myself into and changed the subject.

The next morning, I joined Lucinda and Olivia for St John's church's Christingle service. Whilst I wasn't a believer, I did quite enjoy the traditions of Christmas and the community spirit. I was happy enough sitting through the service with its carols and readings. Olivia and June had their oranges with candles and sticks with fruit stuck in them and a ribbon around them. I knew the orange represented the world and the candle represented light – but I didn't have any idea what the other items signified.

Driving down to Hastings, we broke the journey at Thurrock Services to give the dogs, and the rest of us, a chance to stretch our legs. It was just getting dark and had started raining as we parked on Lucinda's parents' drive. The porch light was already lit showing a seasonal wreath on the front door which opened as I switched off the engine. Olivia already had the dogs' leads on them and jumped out of the car.

"Nanny! Gramps!" she yelled as she ran up to her grandparents, the dogs barking and jumping up at any human they could find.

"Hello darling," her grandmother said, as she wrapped Olivia in her arms and kissed her.

"Don't I get a kiss?" asked her grandad holding his arms wide. Olivia turned and snuggled into his arms.

Lucinda handed her mother a bouquet. While I shook my father-in-law's hand.

"How was the journey, Chris? Much traffic on the M25?" he asked.

"Not too bad, Norman. Usual queues at the Thames crossing," I replied before turning to my mother-in-law. "And how are you, Sylvia?" I asked as we kissed each other's cheeks.

Norman gave me a hand bringing in the luggage while Lucinda and Sylvia made a pot of coffee and Olivia supervised the dogs while they did their business in the back garden.

We carried our drinks into the lounge where the two dogs took up their normal positions, Max lying on the rug in front of the roaring fire and Maya on Olivia's lap. A bare Christmas tree sat in one corner.

"We thought we'd wait until you got here so you could help put up the Christmas decorations, Olivia," her grandmother told her. "We'll do it after dinner."

The holiday went smoothly.

We all attended the midnight service on Christmas Eve. Thankfully, the local vicar wasn't like the fire and brimstone type at St John's. Sitting quietly and thinking to myself while others around me joined in the prayers, I felt jealous of their sense of belonging to a community. Friends in the Gay Village spoke about the trans community but I didn't think it shared the same sense of purpose as the church appeared to have. But, perhaps that was an illusion. Maybe the church had as many schisms in its ranks as the trans and wider LGBT communities. Perhaps all groups shared a key factor but were otherwise disparate. Could it be that all humans had this need to belong to something and chose a group that shared their most important core belief?

The next morning, we opened our presents before dressing. Olivia was particularly pleased with her riding kit, to which her grandparents had added a pair of gloves and a hat, and Lucinda seemed to like the jewellery I gave her. As I unwrapped the shirts she had given me, I imagined how the necklace and earrings would have gone with the dress I'd worn at the face-to-face gathering. In fact, it wouldn't have worked as the earrings were for pierced ears and I really didn't think I could get away with having mine pierced.

Once the presents had been unwrapped, we dressed, then had a light breakfast as we'd be sitting down to a traditional Christmas dinner promptly at half past one so we'd have ample time to eat and clear up the dishes before the Queen's speech on television. No doubt there would be some reference this year to Princess Diana's death a few months ago.

After breakfast on Boxing Day, Norman and I cleared the table and loaded the dishwasher then refilled our coffee cups and took them into the lounge. The house was a substantial Victorian property in a solid area on the northern outskirts of Hastings.

"How are things going in Manchester?" Norman asked. "You seem to spend a lot of time up there."

"The project is going well but I do need to be hands-on. The Managing Director is pleased from what I hear," I told him.

"How do you manage living up there though. I mean it's a lot different to what you're used to, isn't it? Lots of gun crime from what I read in the Daily Mail."

"It's true there are rough areas, but the flat I rent is in a quiet road, so I haven't had problems," I replied – I could hardly mention that I'd had my handbag stolen at traffic lights.

Norman nodded his head.

"Chorlton is one of the more upmarket parts of Manchester. It used to be Conservative until the mid-eighties. Now nearly the whole of Manchester is red with just a couple of lib-dem councillors. I was surprised to see Hastings elect a Labour MP in May, though. But then, Labour did a lot better than most people expected. They even took second place where my parents live – though it did remain Conservative."

Our MP was also a Conservative – in fact, I'd lived in blue territories most of my life; the flat in Chorlton was the first time I'd found myself in Labour territory.

"The whole world is changing. And not always for the better," Normal proclaimed.

"You may have a point, not that there seems to be much difference between this new man Blair and John Major's financial policies. At least he doesn't seem to be set on nationalising everything," I replied.

"Maybe not," admitted Norman begrudgingly. "But just look at the stupid regulations Brussels impose on us. Mark my words, it'll go too far."

My own attitudes had changed since being involved in the scene in Manchester. I'd previously supported most traditional values and had seen the far left, like Michael Foot, as supporting scroungers and wanting to nationalise everything. And it certainly seemed to me that a lot of nationalised industries were inefficient and just holes into which taxpayers' money was tipped.

On the other hand, I recognised that the right wing was bigoted and change was needed. That included changes as far as LGBT issues were concerned. Maggie had prohibited any education about gay issues in schools, there were bans on gay members of the armed forces and no protection for trans people at all. Venues could even refuse to serve LGBT individuals. There was a group fighting for trans rights but I, frankly, didn't hold out much hope – even with the change of government. Not that I'd dare make any comment supporting gay rights without raising suspicions. So, I kept quiet.

The fact was that if I was 'outed' as trans, I could say goodbye to my job.

I'd tried stopping over the years, but the compulsion always returned. The best I could do was to make sure it stayed hidden and keep my two lives totally separate. I finished my coffee then asked if anyone else fancied a brisk walk to blow away the cobwebs.

Chapter 19. On a Diet
1st January 1998

Carol pointed to the bathroom scales, "Come on, let's see what you weigh," she instructed.

She checked the reading. "Fourteen stones. According to this chart, you're overweight. You need to lose at least a stone and a half. That settles it, we both need to diet. You'll have to watch what you eat when you're away. I bet you live off takeaways and rubbish food while you're in Manchester. No more fish and chips here on a Friday evening either."

It was the same every year. We'd stuff ourselves over Christmas then Lucinda would find some of her things were a bit tight so we'd all have to cut back. To be fair, I wanted to lose a bit of weight in any case. I'd seen a couple of dresses I fancied but they weren't available in a size 16. I was quite happy going for healthier options of ready-to-eat meals if that cut out a few calories.

"Now the project is in the build phase, I'm likely to have to spend more time out on site – and walking around in safety gear is good exercise. I might even join a gym up there. That'll also help to lose a few pounds," I said.

"Well, I'll be weighing us every weekend from now on and we'll keep a record. At least Olivia is fine. Her riding and the work she does at the stables gives her plenty of exercise," Lucinda added.

Olivia had really taken to riding and had jumped at the opportunity to muck out the stables and help keep the indoor training ring clean in exchange for extra lessons. She was looking forward to taking part in a local gymkhana in the spring; she took every opportunity to wear the set of jodhpurs, and boots we'd given her for Christmas.

Chapter 20. A Stiff Whisky
Friday 20th February 1998

Claire and Lucinda were spending the spring half-term holiday with the in- aws in Hastings; so, I had two weekends in Manchester. In fact, the first of the weekends coincided with a national trans group weekend in Blackpool. I was sharing with Sara who was coming down from Inverness. We'd kept in touch since she'd stopped with me for the F2F, as the Face-to-Face get-together was now known.

The group had exclusive use of the Palace Hotel on the seafront for the weekend. There was quite a programme planned including a welcome buffet followed by a disco on Friday evening, some talks and demonstrations during the day on Saturday and Sunday and a gala dinner with a live band on the Saturday evening.

I left work at lunchtime as usual on a Friday and returned to the flat to change and pack before driving to Blackpool. It was an easy drive and I arrived at the hotel soon after four pm.

Sara had beaten me to it by a few minutes and was already in our room.

"I've taken the bed next to the window and hung my things up in the right-hand wardrobe," she told me. "Hope that's OK."

It was. I unpacked my outfits then we went down for a drink. As we walked into the bar, we could see that there were already thirty or forty guests. Recognising some of the girls from Manchester, we joined their table. A couple of them were regulars at these weekends.

"Some of the girls will stay in the hotel all weekend, some of us will probably go into town – probably to the Flying Handbag or Flamingos, Basils or Lucy's Bar, rather than just stop for the disco here this evening," Gina explained. "Fancy joining us?"

Sara and I exchanged glances. It was quite a step from the relative security of the Gay Village or going out in daylight to being out on the town in Blackpool amongst straight stag nights and hen parties whose members would be getting drunker as the evening went on.

"What do you think?" asked Sara.

"Let's go for it," I said. I saw her eyes widen as she stared back at me.

Then she closed her eyes and I watched her swallow before she opened them again, grimaced, then say: "OK, but I hope we don't regret it."

"You won't," Gina assured us. "We'll stay here 'til about ten thirty to support the disco for a while then get a cab to Talbot Square. We'll see if Deana is on in Basils, if not we'll go round to Lucy's Bar."

Other girls, recognising Sara and me from the F2F, came and joined us and reminisced over that weekend and asked when the next one was planned. The bar was getting more and more crowded. Looking round, there was a fantastic range of outfits.

One of the girls was in a full ball gown; another in a bride's dress complete with veil, a couple were dressed as young girls, some in schoolgirl's uniforms. There were French maids, nuns and tarts and mini-skirts that were more like belts. Sara and I looked quite demure with our 'girl next door' look. I noticed one girl who seemed to appear in one outfit then disappear for a while before reappearing in a different dress.

"That's Patti-Anne," Gina told me. "She's known for the number of outfits she brings to these weekends."

About seven o'clock, Sara and I decided to go and change for the evening. I had the outfit I'd worn for the F2F dinner – the cerise calf-length A-line dress with boat neckline; Sara had her scarlet, mid-thigh length, dress. I felt that we showed style rather than glitziness. The buffet had started by the time we got back downstairs so we helped ourselves and found a table and bought drinks from the bar.

The DJ had already started playing and the dance floor was filling as a mix of sixties, seventies and eighties tracks were belted out.

As we danced later, I thought about how Philip and I had danced together. How it had felt with his body pressed against mine; how his lips had felt kissing me. I did miss having sex with him. But I accepted that I couldn't give him − nor any gay man − what he wanted. I certainly couldn't give a straight guy what he wanted either unless I had surgery and that was not something I would even consider.

"I've ordered a taxi for ten-thirty,' Gina reminded Sara and me. I checked my watch, in fifteen minutes.

"Fine, I'm going to use the loo and get a jacket," I told her. "I'll meet you at reception."

It was only a short drive from the hotel to Talbot Square where the cab dropped us. I was very glad we didn't have far to walk to the club as there was a bitter wind blowing in off the Irish Sea. We nodded to the doorman at the entrance to Basils then climbed the stairs and left our jackets in the cloakroom.

As we walked into the dance floor, the flamboyant DJ saw us.

"Ah, the tranny weekend is in town. Come in girls. Welcome to the best show in town. How are you doing Gina?" she called.

Gina walked straight over to the DJ box and they air-kissed. She signalled to us to join them.

"This is Deana, she claims to be the best DJ in town; but that's only since I stopped performing. This is Chris and Sara and you already know Kath."

"Hi girls, just a second," she turned to her decks and introduced the next track, before returning her attention to us.

We stayed in Basils for an hour then walked round the corner to Lucy's Bar for even more dancing. As I stood to one side having a drink, I could see Sara with her arms wrapped around a guy's neck, his hand pressing her bum and pressing his body against hers. As they turned, she looked over his shoulder at me and winked. I knew what she was feeling and wasn't at all surprised to see them kissing a few seconds later.

As the record finished, Sara came over to me, holding her partner's hand in hers.

"I'm going back to Tony's hotel with him, I'll see you in the morning," she told me.

"OK, have fun – but stay safe," I said. I was concerned about her going off with him, but it was her choice.

We left Lucy's Bar about two and picked up a taxi at a nearby rank. There were still a few girls chatting in the bar when we got back to our hotel so we joined them for a final nightcap.

The next morning, I checked my phone for any messages from Sara – but there were none. I wasn't particularly surprised but it didn't stop me worrying. I dressed then went down for breakfast. Gina and Kath were already at a table so I joined them.

"No Sara this morning?" asked Gina.

"No, she went off with that guy Tony that she met in Lucy's," I replied.

"Dirty stop-out," remarked Kath.

"You're just jealous," Gina told her.

"True. So, Chris, what are your plans for this morning; well, what's left of it?"

"I want to have a look around the displays and attend the hair removal talk at eleven. I also want to check out the wigs and get some tips from the make-up girl. Sara and I were going shopping this afternoon, but I guess that depends on what time she gets back. If she gets back and doesn't decide to spend the day with Tony."

"We're planning to go to the Pleasure Beach, you're welcome to join us. We're going to have a ride on the tram now. You ready, Gina?"

"See you later, Chris," Gina said as she stood up and slung her bag over her shoulder.

There wasn't time to do much else before the talk I wanted to attend so I poured myself another cup of coffee and smoked a cigarette.

The talk on different forms of electrolysis was very interesting. I'd never wanted a moustache or beard and it would certainly make sense to remove as much hair as I could. It would make it a lot easier to hide five o'clock shadow. I then had a makeover with the girl explaining the techniques she was using and giving me advice on colours that suited me best. Obviously, I had to buy the foundation, lipstick, blusher and eye-shadow she was recommending. At least my usual mascara was OK.

The shoe stand focussed on exotic and fetishistic boots and shoes; most with at least four-inch stiletto heels. They did have some more normal court shoes and sandals – and I was very tempted to buy a pair of strappy evening shoes with three-inch heels that would go perfectly with the dress I had for the gala dinner. My budget didn't allow for both the shoes and a wig I also wanted to buy and, in the end, the shoes lost out. I did take a note of the style and the website address.

Sara had still not turned up when I dropped off my purchases in our room. It was pouring with rain so I decided against going into town. I touched up my make-up then went back downstairs. There were some more activities that the organisers had arranged in the ballroom and plenty of people to talk to.

As I came out of the lift, Rita, one of the organisers, signalled me to join her and a woman standing with her. Rita looked very concerned. I immediately thought something must have happened to Sara.

"Chris, this is Detective Sergeant Shaw, she needs to speak to you," Rita said.

"Is it about Sara?" I asked.

"Perhaps we can discuss this privately? Would you come with me, please?" DS Shaw remarked.

I followed her into a side room off the reception area. She invited me to sit down then took a chair herself.

"In answer to your question, yes, this relates to Sara Campbell. I believe you were sharing a room with her. How well do you know her?"

"She stayed at my flat in Manchester for another event and we've chatted by phone but I don't know her that well. Why? What's happened to her? Is she OK?"

"I'm sorry to tell you that she was attacked last night and is in a very serious condition in hospital."

So, my fears had proved justified.

"Will she be all right? Which hospital is she in? What happened?" I asked.

"She's in Blackpool Victoria and the staff are doing all they can. I'm hoping you can help us put together what happened to her. She staggered into the reception of a hotel near Central Pier and collapsed. She'd been stabbed. The night porter called for an ambulance and did what he could to stop the bleeding."

"Who did it?" I asked. I hardly needed to ask 'why'. Trans people are frequently targets; just for being who we are.

"That's what we need to find out. When and where did you last see her?"

"We went to a couple of clubs off Talbot Square. Sara was dancing with a guy in Lucy's and said she was going back to his hotel with him."

"Which hotel? What time was this?"

"I've no idea which hotel it was. I guess the time was between midnight and one. I didn't take any notice, to be honest. We stayed until the club closed then caught a cab back here. That would have been about two am."

"You say 'we' – who else was with you?"

I gave her Gina's and Kath's names which she wrote in her notebook.

"Who was the man Sara left with? Can you describe him? Would you recognise him again?"

I thought for a moment; trying hard to picture him.

"His name was Tony – no idea what his surname was. He was a little taller than me so say about five-ten, medium build, not slim but not overweight; short brown hair; but not very short – kind of smart military look? I didn't notice his eyes but he was clean-shaven. I think I'd be able to identify him."

"How was he dressed? What about his accent?"

"I didn't speak to him except to say 'hi' when Sara introduced him but I didn't notice any pronounced accent. He was dressed smart casual, open-necked button-through plain coloured shirt, yellowy-green, I think. Difficult to tell in the club lighting. Dark grey trousers, not jeans. Ordinary shoes, not trainers, and they were well polished. Do you think he might have been the one who attacked Sara?"

"Thanks. At the moment, we're trying to piece together her movements and identify anyone who was with her last night. We need you to come down to the station this afternoon to make a formal statement; would that be a problem for you?"

Shit. This could get awkward. What if they wanted my real name and address? What if they wrote to me there?

DS Shaw obviously picked up on my hesitation.

"Look, I realise this could be difficult for you – but we'll try to be as discrete as possible and I'm sure you don't want her attacker to get away with it, do you?"

"Of course not. But I don't know anything about the actual attack."

"No, but if you can identify this 'Tony', that'll help us. Just ask at the desk for DC Hannah Reid, she'll take your statement and possibly ask you to look through some photo albums. Now, where can I find Gina and Kath?"

"They went to the pleasure beach but should be back later," I told her.

Dazed, unable to take it in, I wandered into the bar and ordered a stiff whisky. I shouldn't have left Sara last night. But, could anyone have stopped her going off with Tony? She knew the risks – just like when I first went with Philip. But what can you do? The options are to avoid all encounters or take the chance. Even using public transport or walking down the street was a risk. It went with the territory.

I sank the whisky in one gulp – then went to my room and phoned the hospital.

I had to pretend to be Sara's brother to get any information about her. There was no chance that any other member of her family would be phoning – she'd told me that they'd disowned her when she transitioned.

The news wasn't good. She was in Intensive Care and in a critical condition. I was invited to phone back later in the day for an update. As dinner wasn't until eight that evening and lunch had finished, I went out to a nearby café.

After a snack, I caught the tram into the town centre and reported to the police station to make my statement. One or two eyebrows were lifted and I noticed some smirks as I was taken into an interview room – but DC Reid was fine with me and happy to accept the flat address and my 'Christine' mobile for the contact details. She left me to look through some photo albums to see if I could pick out Tony while she went to fetch me a coffee.

"Forget those, Chris," she announced on her return. She showed me a photo ID. "Is this Tony?"

"Yes, that's him."

"I'm afraid he's dead. His body was behind a skip in a back alley a few hundred yards from the hotel Sara reached."

"How will this affect the investigation? Will I still be involved? Do you still need my statement?" I'd been prepared to help but it didn't now sound as though any information I could give was relevant.

"Probably not, unless we still need to prove a link between him and Sara when it comes to trial. This is now a murder enquiry so the decision will be well above my level."

"So, what happened?" I asked. "Were they both attacked?"

"That's certainly one line of investigation. Maybe Sara can help us when she recovers. If she recovers. I've just been on to the hospital and she's still very poorly. By the way, the hospital says they had an enquiry from someone claiming to be her brother. You wouldn't know anything about that would you?"

I looked sheepishly at her.

"Sorry, yes. I was concerned about her and my voice sounds too deep to claim to be her sister."

"OK, that clears that up – at least I don't have to try to find the mystery caller."

Pausing outside the police station to light a cigarette and check the time, I wondered if I should return to the hotel or take a taxi to the hospital to visit Sara. Would they let me see her? Was she allowed visitors? Was she still unconscious or had she come around?

Overhead, gulls screeched as they searched for easy targets to dive-bomb for chips. The cold wind off the sea made me pull my jacket tighter. Horns and sirens sounded over the background cacophony of vehicle engines – engines that were pumping out stinking exhaust fumes. Not that I could really comment as smoke from my cigarette added to the pollution.

In spite of the risk of a wasted trip, but knowing I wouldn't relax until I knew how she was, I picked up a cab at a rank on Talbot Square.

Having paid off the taxi at the entrance to the hospital, I looked around at ambulances arriving with their two-tones wailing and blue lights flashing in the dusk. Paramedics transferred patients on trolleys, crashing through the doors into A&E.

I passed through the main entrance and found an enquiry desk. The receptionist couldn't give me any information about Sara's condition but directed me to the ICU where a nurse pointed out Sara's bed in a side ward. At least I then knew she was still alive. As I approached her bed, I saw her eyes open and her face lit up with a smile as she saw me.

"Hi Chris, lovely to see you," she said.

I leant over and kissed her forehead.

"How are you doing? I've been so worried about you," I told her as I looked around.

She seemed to be connected to an array of instruments and had a drip-feeding fluid into her arm. I could see she was bandaged round her midriff – the outline visible through her hospital gown.

"Sore," she said. "I have this stabbing pain in my side."

It was good to see she hadn't lost her sense of humour.

"What do the doctors say? Have they said how long you're likely to be in for?" I asked.

"They say I'm out of danger but need to monitor me for another day or so. Seems that although I lost a lot of blood, there were no internal injuries."

"That's a relief. We were all concerned. I've been to the police station to make a statement. Not that I could tell them very much. I came straight here afterwards. So, what happened?"

"We were near Tony's hotel when three thugs laid into us calling Tony a faggot and abusing him for going out with a she-male. Tony tried to get between them and me but one of them stabbed me before Tony could stop him. Then they all turned on him. I wanted to help but he shouted to me to go for assistance and he backed off down the street then ran into an alleyway. I was bleeding badly but saw the entrance to a hotel so staggered into it then collapsed. Next thing I knew, I woke up in here. Do you know what happened to Tony? Is he all right? No one here seems to know."

I think she could tell from my face that it wasn't good news.

"He's dead, isn't he?" she asked.

"Yes," I confirmed. "I'm so sorry."

She turned her head and looked down. I could see tears forming at the corner of her eyes then she wiped them away.

"He saved my life, but it cost him his own."

There wasn't anything I could say, so I said nothing.

"Is there anything I can do for you? Anything you want or need?" I asked after a few moments.

"Could you possibly bring my things from the hotel? Doesn't look like I'll be leaving here before our room booking runs out."

"Of course, I can. I'll bring them over tomorrow." I then had a thought.

"Look, are you going to be OK travelling back to Inverness when they discharge you from here? Why don't you come back to Manchester for a few days first?"

"I don't know when that'll be. Could be Monday, might be Tuesday — or later still."

"No problem. It's only forty-five minutes each way. I can come back up after work and collect you."

"Are you sure? That would be marvellous. Thanks."

At that, she was looking past me; I turned round and saw a tall man in a sports jacket and grey trousers standing at the foot of her bed.

"Can I have a word with you, Miss Campbell?" There had been a sarcastic stress on the 'Miss'. "I'm Detective Constable Anderson. It's about the murder of Anthony Cooper."

"She's only just learned that Tony is dead and she's seriously ill herself; can't this wait a day or two?" I asked.

He looked me up and down a sneer appearing on his face.

"And who are you, sir?" he demanded. "It is 'sir' isn't it? Is this any of your business?"

Technically sir was correct in my case – but no less offensive for that.

I glared at him and was about to respond when Sara intervened.

"It's OK, Chris. I'd rather get it over with. You get back to the hotel and enjoy the evening – make sure you take lots of photos so I can see what I missed. I'll see you tomorrow."

Chapter 21. Blackpool Rock
Saturday 21st February 1998

There was a torrential downpour as I left the hospital but, fortunately, a taxi had just dropped off a fare and I was able to jump in and ask to be taken back to the hotel.

Rita caught me as I entered the foyer.

"Have you heard anything more about Sara?" she asked.

"I've just been to the hospital; she's not too bad but they're keeping her under observation for a couple more days."

"Oh, thank God. We had been wondering about the gala dinner – some of the members wondered if it would have been insensitive to continue with it if she'd been…"

Rita seemed to be struggling with how to complete the sentence.

"Dead?" I suggested.

"Well, yes, or even still in a critical condition."

"Thankfully, that's not the case and she wants us to go ahead with the dinner and take lots of photos to show her what she's missed."

Rita was clearly very relieved. If the gala dinner had been cancelled, there would have been some guests who would have asked about refunds.

I excused myself and went up to the room to have a bath and change.

The gala dinner entertainment featured 'The Blackpool Rockers' a 60s tribute band. My dress for the evening was A line with a round neck; the sleeveless bodice was plain black and the flared skirt had black polka dots on a white background; the belt had a bow on the left hip. Black three-inch stilettos completed the outfit. I thought it went perfectly with the event theme.

The evening started with a 'Champagne Reception' – except it wasn't Champagne but Cava; not that I minded; I preferred Cava, Champagne was usually too dry for my palate. I picked up a glass, took a sip and looked around the room. The hotel had done a fabulous job and the tables, each for 8, were beautifully decorated and arranged around a dance floor that would be filled later.

The DJ was playing the Tornado's Telstar – as it faded away, he invited us to take our seats as dinner was about to be served. Finding my place, I said hello to the others who had already taken their places. Thankfully, Kath and Gina were on the same table but I didn't know the other four guests. Sara's place remained empty, of course.

"What's this?" I asked – holding up a small stick of rock that was on my plate.

"It's a traditional 'calling card' gimmick for the Blackpool Rockers. They have sticks made with their names and phone number all the way through. The drummer Wayne's dad owns a rock factory," Gina told me.

"Clever idea," I acknowledged. "I'll take Sara's to her when I visit tomorrow."

"How about introductions. I'm Chris, I know Gina and Kath but don't think we've met before," I said to the other four at our table.

"I'm Gloria," said the one sitting next to Gina.

"Diane, hi," said the next with a wave of her hand.

"Hazel," added the next – raising her glass to me.

"And I'm Phyllis," said the other. "Are you the one sharing with the girl who was stabbed?"

"That's right. Glad to say she's much better but they're keeping her in for observations for a couple more days."

My comments were made irrelevant a moment later when Rita stepped up to the stage and picked up a microphone that she tapped before making her announcement.

"I usually take this opportunity to welcome everyone and outline the plans for the evening – but, this evening, I want to bring you all up to date on the attack on one of our members. As most of you know, our sister Sara was attacked and seriously injured last night and is in hospital. Chris visited her this afternoon and we're pleased to hear that she is out of danger. Tragically, her companion, Tony, was less fortunate and was murdered defending Sara. Let's all stand in silence for a moment in respect."

The sound of chair legs scraping along the floor quickly subsided and I stood thinking about the bigotry that left us so vulnerable. I knew that trans people were about twenty times more likely to be murdered than the average person; that four out of five had experienced verbal abuse and nearly every trans person lost their job when transitioning. It was a sobering thought.

Thankfully, the atmosphere lightened as the waiting staff served our first course. The choice had been between egg mayonnaise with triangles of brown bread or leak and potato soup. I'd ordered the egg mayo.

While we ate, the DJ played a selection of 60s ballads with a few 80s and 90s tracks thrown in for the younger members of the group.

"So, do you all know each other?" I asked as the waitress removed our starter plates. "Have you been to many of these events before?"

"This is my seventh year," Phyllis announced. "Gloria came to the third one I attended and we've come together since then."

"This my second time," said Hazel.

"My first," added Diane. "What about you?"

"My first too," I said.

"Really?" queried Gloria. "You look very experienced; do you dress much then? Or are you TS?"

"No, I'm not transsexual but, yes, I do dress a lot. I work away from home and have a flat in Manchester. I usually change as soon as I get in from work," I said, wondering if I'd revealed too much.

"Wow, lucky girl. I bet you go down the Village a lot too. I wish I could do the same," said Gloria.

"Yes, I do go to the Village; usually on a Wednesday night to Northern Concord but also at the weekend if I don't go home."

"I take it you're married then. Doesn't your wife know about your dressing?" asked Diane.

I lit a cigarette before replying.

"Yes, I am and no, she doesn't know. I don't think she'd be at all happy if she did."

"Why not? You're not doing anything illegal and it doesn't hurt anyone. I bet she sometimes wears trousers – so why shouldn't we be allowed to wear dresses? It's hypocritical to object," Hazel interjected.

The conversation was interrupted by the arrival of our main course. My poached salmon with new potatoes and broccoli looked fabulous. I took a sip of my wine, a crisp Australian Chardonnay, before slicing into the salmon.

As we ate, the others quizzed me about Manchester's Gay Village and the venues and how tranny friendly they were as they'd heard of it but never visited. I told them about my favourites and recommended a couple of hotels to stay in if they visited the area. Finally, I forked the last piece of salmon into my mouth, laid down my utensils, washed the morsel down with the wine then refilled my glass from the bottle I'd intended to share with Sara. Not that I'd have any difficulty drinking it all.

After coffee had been served, the waitresses cleared the tables and the band took their place on the stage.

A Cliff Richard look-alike took hold of the microphone as the percussionist silenced the room with a drum roll.

"Are you all ready to have fun?" he asked.

There was a muted response.

"I said, are you ready to have fun?" he repeated.

This time there was a much more enthusiastic response.

"That's more like it. We're the Blackpool Rockers and we're going to rock this place tonight!"

He nodded to the drummer who tapped his sticks against the drum to lead them into the first number 'Living Doll'.

The dance floor quickly filled as we abandoned our tables and started dancing to the music.

A quick selection of Cliff Richard classics morphed into a selection of Elvis, Beatles, Dave Clark Five, Buddy Holly and others from the 50s and 60s. At various intervals, girls from the audience would join the band to give their impression of Lulu, Shirley Bassey, Cilla Black, Helen Shapiro and Susan Maughan.

The music was earlier than my own era but it clearly went down well with nearly everyone as few stayed at their tables. Eventually, however, it was time for the last dance before I retreated with tired feet to my room.

The next morning, I packed my own case then sorted Sara's items into two piles – one to take to the hospital for her, the other to take back to Manchester with me.

Chapter 22. Full English
Sunday 22nd February 1998

In spite of the glass of Cava, the best part of two bottles of wine and a Tia Maria with my coffee, my head wasn't too bad when I woke on Sunday morning. I showered, applied my make-up, then dressed in a knee-length navy blue skirt and lighter blue jumper.

The dining room was relatively quiet; clearly some of the other guests were having a lie-in. Perhaps their heads were worse than mine this morning. I didn't recognise anyone and rather than join others who were already eating, I took a table to myself near the window. Rain was lashing the other side of the glass – driven off the Irish Sea across the promenade by gusty winds. It wasn't a day for the beach. In fact, if I was at home in Cambridgeshire, I'd be lighting a log fire and sitting reading or, perhaps, playing a board game with Olivia.

I looked around the room. Fewer than half the guests were dressed en femme; most were in male mode; no doubt they'd be checking out and heading home after breakfast. It was strange trying to work out who they'd been the night before.

"Would you care to order, madam?" asked a waitress, who had come over to my table, interrupting my musing.

"I'll have the full English, please, with scrambled eggs – no beans or mushrooms, thank you," I told her. "And coffee please."

She returned a few minutes later and filled my cup with the coffee I'd ordered. It wasn't long before she was back with a rack of toast and I buttered half a slice and took a bite to keep me going until the main breakfast arrived. When it did, the plate was well loaded with two rashers of bacon, a sausage, grilled tomato and scrambled eggs.

It may not have been particularly lady-like, but I attacked it with gusto.

I finished with another cup of coffee and smoked a cigarette while I thought about the day ahead. Sara and I had planned to take the tram along the coast to the shopping outlet at Fleetwood but that didn't appeal to me anymore. In any event, I now needed to pack my own case and sort Sara's clothes into two bags – one to take to her at the hospital, the other to take back to my flat. If the rain didn't ease – and it looked like it had settled in for the day – the drive back down the M61 was going to be tedious and it would be sensible to do it before it got dark.

At the hospital, I called at the shop near the entrance and bought some chocolates, biscuits and copies of Cosmopolitan, Vogue, Marie Claire and Private Eye which I hoped Sara would like. I thought of buying some flowers too – but realised I'd struggle to carry them as well as my handbag, the carrier bag containing the magazines etc and the bag with her clothes.

As I entered the side ward where Sara's bed was, I saw that DC Anderson was standing over her. Her face was flushed and she was pursing her lips as she stared, defiantly, at him.

"So, you expect me to believe that you and your boyfriend did nothing to cause the assault on you?"

"Of course not. We were just walking along together and they attacked us," Sara protested.

"Walking along? Holding hands, no doubt?" the DC mocked.

"What if we were holding hands? What's wrong with that? It's not illegal."

"It may not be illegal but some people find it offensive and react against it."

"So, you're saying we brought it on ourselves. Is that it?"

"I'm not saying anything. But, if you didn't prance around in female clothes and come on to guys, maybe it wouldn't have happened."

I felt my fists clenching and had to control an urge to punch him.

"Is that what YOU think DC Anderson?" I asked.

He turned and noticed me for the first time. He looked me up and down as though I was something to scrape off his shoes.

"Well, SIR, it doesn't really matter what I think. But it may be that the defendants, if they are traced, will use that in their defence and, believe me, some judges share that view too. Oh, we know that Blackpool attracts queers and trannies because of some of the clubs – but it used to be a wholesome family resort – not a place for perverts."

Sara was waving her hand at me and shaking her head while Anderson was looking in my direction. I took the hint and swallowed the response I'd been about to utter. There was nothing to be gained by pointing out that being transgender was perfectly natural; that Sara identified as female so there was nothing perverted about her wanting to be with a man – or asking why anyone was entitled to object to same-sex couples in any case.

"By the way, MISTER Williamson, I'll need your full real name and home address in case we need to get in touch with you – and your date of birth," Anderson continued.

"Why do you need my date of birth?"

"We need to check whether or not you have a record on the Police National Computer."

"What on earth for? I'm not a suspect. My only involvement is as a friend of one of the victims and having seen Tony in the club. I've already given a statement to your Sergeant who was quite happy to accept my Manchester address."

It was quite obvious that his reason was simply to make me worry about the possibility of being outed.

"Are you refusing to cooperate in the investigation of the alleged offence? Obstructing the police is a serious offence itself. SIR."

"I've given you all the information I can about the matter so I doubt that you can charge me with obstructing the police. But, if you think you can, then let's discuss it with your Sergeant."

He pursed his lips and stared at me while he appeared to be considering my response. I returned his stare. Eventually, he turned to look at Sara.

"I think we have all we need from you for the time being. We'll be in touch if there are any further developments or if we need further information from you."

He turned, sneering at me as he pushed past me and left the room.

"Bastard," I remarked. "How dare he speak to us like that?"

"Goes with the territory, Chris. We have no real protection against bigotry; though there has been a case in the European Court of Justice that says the Sex Discrimination Act covers transsexuals. As far as I can see, it only covers employment though, not discrimination like our friend Anderson."

"That's so wrong. What harm are you, or I, doing? We don't hurt anyone else, why should we have to put up with bigotry?" I asked. "Anyway," I continued, trying to change the mood, "I've brought you a bag with toiletries and a change of clothes – and a few magazines for you to read. Oh and a few nibbles to keep you going in case the food in here leaves something to be desired. Your mobile charger is in the bag too."

"That's lovely, thanks, Chris. You're a good friend."

"Have they said when you might be discharged?"

"Not before Tuesday."

"OK, well, send me an SMS when you know for certain. I'll come and pick you up after work. It'll probably be about seven, seven-thirty by the time I pop back to the flat to change. Is that OK?"

"Perfect. There's probably somewhere I can wait if they kick me out before then because they need my bed," Sara replied. I was glad to see she still had her sense of humour. Her eyelids were beginning to droop; perhaps Anderson had been more of a strain on her than I'd realised.

"I'd better be on my way and let you get some rest," I told her.

She took my hand in hers and squeezed it as I leant over and kissed her on the forehead.

"I'll see you when you're ready to come out," I said.

I gave her a final wave as I went out of the door – but her eyes were already closed.

As arranged, I returned to collect Sara when she was discharged on the Tuesday and took her back to my flat in Manchester so she could recover sufficiently for the much longer journey back to Inverness. Against her protests, I gave up my bed and slept on the sofa and tried to disturb her as little as possible when getting ready for work in the morning.

When I got back from the office on Wednesday, Sara had prepared a meal for us.

"I've thrown a few things together that I found in the fridge and freezer for dinner; it'll be ready in half an hour," she told me.

"Smells delicious. You'll make someone a fabulous wife," I said. "I'll just go and change," I added.

She was just putting the casserole dish on the table as I returned after changing into a skirt and blouse. She removed the apron she'd been wearing round her waist and scooped her skirt from underneath her legs as she sat down.

I opened a bottle of wine and poured some for each of us and we chinked glasses and took a sip before focussing on the meal.

I tasted the sauce in which the other ingredients were swimming. It was fabulous with hints of different herbs and spices but none of them coming through as the most powerful. The meat would have fallen off the bone had there been any bones in the dish – but it melted in the mouth.

"This is incredible," I told Sara.

"Glad you like it. It's the least I can do for you after your hospitality," she answerec with a smile.

I didn't hesitate when Sara offered me a second helping as I cleared my plate of the first serving. When that had gone the way of the first, I started to get up to make some coffee but she was already rising from her chair and pressed down on my shoulder; squeezing it at the same time.

"You stay there, I'll do it. I've hardly done anything all day," she instructed. "Better still, why don't you go through to the lounge? I'll bring it through in a minute," she added. "Take the rest of the wine through with you."

"Tonight's the Northern Concord meeting," I told her. "Do you fancy going there later?"

"I don't really feel up to it; I'd prefer a quiet night in," she said. "But don't let me stop you going, Chris, if that's what you want to do."

Her words might be saying one thing – but her eyes told a different story.

"No, I'm quite happy staying in for once. I had enough gallivanting around at the weekend for one week."

The layout of the lounge meant that the sofa was the best place to watch the television so we sat down together. Sara leaned forward and poured the coffee into our cups then slid mine along the coffee table before picking up hers and taking a sip.

She suddenly put her cup down on the table again, stood up and rushed out of the lounge. The next thing I heard was her being sick in the bathroom. I followed her and found her bent over the toilet as another wave of vomiting hit her. I rubbed the small of her back and her shoulders to try and comfort her.

"Maybe you shouldn't have drunk that wine," I suggested, jokingly – though I suspected she was actually suffering from delayed shock.

Eventually, she straightened up. I passed her a warm wet flannel to clean her face followed by a glass of water. She gave me a wan half-smile.

"Thanks, I'm not sure what hit me," she whispered.

"I'd have thought it was quite obvious. You've been through a very nasty time and it's not surprising if there are consequences. Come and sit down again in the lounge unless you think you're going to be sick again?"

"No," she said, "I feel better now."

I put my arm around her waist to support her and helped her back to the sofa. She still looked delicate.

"Do you want to talk about it?" I asked. We'd skirted around the subject of the attack until then – but maybe she needed to work through it.

"What, are you going to ask how it makes me feel?" she asked. "That's what my counsellor always asked."

"I'm no counsellor," I told her, "But, I am a good listener and if you want to talk, then maybe it'll help."

"No, I'm fine," she said. I raised my eyebrows and she dropped her gaze to the floor.

"Your choice," I reminded her. "We can just watch TV if that's what you want."

I looked at her and she returned my look.

"I just feel so guilty. Tony's dead and it's my fault. He could have got away but he stopped to protect me and they killed him. Maybe DC Anderson was right, maybe it was our fault for flaunting ourselves. Maybe if we hadn't, they wouldn't have started to call us names; then Tony wouldn't have responded and they'd have left us alone."

Tears flowed down Sara's cheeks and she sobbed uncontrollably. I took her in my arms and stroked her hair as I held her against me.

"Let it out Sara," I told her.

She eventually relaxed but didn't move from my shoulder. Her sobs gradually slowed. I kissed her gently on the forehead, just as I would do with Olivia when comforting her.

"You're a good friend Chris," she said as she sat up. I simply smiled.

"Do you really think it's your fault that Tony's dead?" I asked.

"No, not really."

"Not 'really'?" I challenged. "In what way could ANY responsibility be down to you? What were you doing that gave them any right to take offence?"

"Just holding hands."

"And, why shouldn't a woman hold hands with a man – even in their bigoted view of the world? Because that's what you are isn't it?"

"Well, yes. Of course, I am."

"And were you flaunting yourselves or just minding your own business?"

"We were just walking along."

"So, what gave them any right to object to your behaviour?"

"Nothing, I suppose."

"So how is Tony's death your fault?"

"In my head, I know it wasn't but it doesn't stop me feeling I should have done something to help him."

"And, what could you have done? You'd already been stabbed. If you'd stayed to help, isn't it likely that you'd have died too?"

"I know what you're saying is right but it doesn't make it any easier or make me less scared of ever going out again at night."

"That I can totally understand," I told her. "But maybe it's like falling off a horse. Maybe you need to get back in the saddle – or, in this case, go out for an evening somewhere relatively safe. Maybe like the Village."

Sara leaned across and kissed me lightly on the cheek.

"Thanks. I've said it before, but you're a really good friend."

The arm I'd comforted her with was still around her shoulder and she seemed content to leave it there as she snuggled against me.

After a few minutes, Sara reached for the bottle of wine and topped up our glasses before passing me mine and settling back on the sofa. She could have created some space between us but, instead, she sat back as she'd been before, our sides touching. I'd left my arm resting along the back of the sofa so it was still around her shoulder.

"I feel safer with your arm around me," she said. "You don't mind, do you?"

"Of course not," I replied, giving her shoulder a squeeze.

She rested her hand on my knee. "Good," she said.

I wondered if it was just safety she felt or if she was looking for more. I was confused. At first, I'd comforted her as a friend; but having her in my arms, smelling her perfume and feeling her soft hair, it had become more than that. I was tempted to kiss her and wondered how she'd react. Her hand on my knee suggested she wouldn't object.

But, if I did, where would that lead? And what were the implications?

Was I fancying Sara as a guy fancies a girl? In spite of wearing a skirt and blouse and female undies, I was a guy. I definitely saw Sara as female; that was obvious. But did she see me as male or female? She'd been planning to go to bed with Tony so clearly fancied men but, apart from when I got back from work, she'd only seen me as female.

What if I'd misread the situation and Sara didn't want me to kiss her? How embarrassing would that be? How would Sara feel then? She still wasn't fit to travel but would she still feel able to stay in the flat? I doubted if I would be in her place.

Shit, what a mess.

I drank the last of my wine, then leant forward to reach for the bottle but it was empty.

"Do you fancy a top-up, Sara? I can always open another bottle?" I asked.

"Why not?" she responded.

When I returned to the lounge with the fresh bottle of Merlot, Sara had moved away from where I'd left her and there was clear space between us when I sat down again. She'd lit a cigarette and I did the same before picking up the remote control, switching on the television and surfing through the channels.

"Anything you fancy? Or there's some video tapes."

Sara put her glass down on the table, rested her cigarette in the ashtray then stood up and walked over to the TV stand and checked out the tapes stored in the drawers.

"Priscilla, Queen of the Desert? The Birdcage? Rocky Horror Picture Show? To Wong Foo, Thanks for the Memories?" she read out, "Do I detect a theme here?"

"There are others," I said, in my defence; not all of them had transgender themes.

"True, you've got Trainspotting, Boogie Nights, Schindler's List, and Just Like a Woman. Ah Julie Walters, now she's good. Let's try this one."

She took out the tape and inserted it into the letterbox flap of the video recorder while I selected the appropriate input for the TV.

As the initial credits and advertisements for other films played, Sara returned to the sofa and sat down again.

The initial scenes as Geraldine's wife finds him surrounded by female attire and, believing him to be having an affair, throws him out, remind me of the risks I take and the consequences I'd probably face if I was discovered. I recognise, too, the surreptitious manner in which he has to sneak around Monica's house when lodging with her. Her acceptance of

Geraldine when she eventually discovers the truth is probably most transvestites' dream but one that few imagine could ever come true.

I feel for Geraldine when she's stopped by the police while driving through London and how they become very insulting when they realise she's a transvestite. Sara's hand reached for mine at that point.

"Bastards!" she exclaimed. "Just like that pig Anderson in Blackpool."

When Geraldine is fired because of being trans, Sara purses her lips and grits her teeth.

"Why should she be fired? What difference does it make to how she can do her job – or how he can do his job, however they see themselves. It really pisses me off," she said.

She relaxed more as the plot developed; squeezing my hand as Monica persuades Geraldine to expose the underhand plans of his former employer to cheat a Japanese client by attending a meeting as Geraldine – with the predictable conclusion that she wins the day.

"I enjoyed that," Sara said as the end credits rolled up the screen. She then seemed to notice that she was still holding my hand. And that I hadn't stopped her. She gave it a squeeze and I responded.

She then gathered up the coffee cups and wine glasses, took them into the kitchen and washed them – leaving them to dry on the draining rack. Meanwhile, I started to make up the sofa as my bed.

"I was wondering," she said, as she came back into the lounge, "I'm still feeling a bit shaky, I don't suppose you'd sleep with me tonight – just to hold me, nothing else. I'd just feel safer if you did. But, if you wouldn't feel comfortable doing that, then I understand."

I knew we were entering dangerous territory but I took her hands in mine, looked her in the eyes and said "If that's what you want, then, of course I'll sleep with you." I tried to lighten the situation by adding "But only on condition that you don't try to take advantage of me."

In the bed, Sara lay on her side facing away from me and I snuggled up to her back. I rested my hand on her stomach, away from any erotic zones, and she held it there. My face pressed into her hair and I could smell the delicate feminine fragrance of her shampoo.

Within minutes, her breathing slowed and deepened as she fell asleep; a gentle burbling sound escaping from her lips as she exhaled.

The next morning, Sara got out of bed at the same time as me and put her wrap on over her nightdress.

"What do you want for breakfast?" she asked.

"I usually have cereal and toast, but don't worry I can get it myself," I replied.

"Nonsense, I'll get it sorted while you have your shower and dress."

I ate my breakfast and had a cigarette with my coffee before gathering up my briefcase and getting ready to leave.

"I thought I could do some laundry while you're at work. Is there anywhere to hang the clothes to dry – I hate using tumble driers unless absolutely necessary."

"I just hang my smalls in the bathroom but there is a rotary line near the gate to the parking spaces," I told her.

"Was there anything you'd like for dinner? Are there any shops nearby?" she asked.

"There's a few shops on the High Street at the end of the road if you do want anything. But, don't go to any trouble for me though."

"It's no trouble. I'll need a bit of fresh air and exercise and I enjoy cooking."

"Becoming quite the housewife, aren't you?" I joked.

"Well, just taking advantage of the opportunity. Don't imagine I'll ever find a guy who wants to settle down with a woman with my history. Oh,

I know it happens sometimes but very much the exception. You don't mind, do you?"

"Not at all. It's nice to be looked after."

Sara walked with me to the door. As I turned and said, "See you this evening then." She leant forward and kissed me on the lips.

"Bye, love, have a good day at the office." There was a twinkle in her eyes but I wasn't sure if she was just teasing or if she was exploring boundaries.

I struggled to concentrate all day. My mind kept returning to the questions I'd been asking myself when we'd been sitting on the sofa.

I thought I'd got my life reasonably well compartmentalised. As Christopher, I was Lucinda's husband and Olivia's father. As Christine, I was female and what happened in that life was separate from when I was male. But, now, there was Sara. I liked Sara. I fancied Sara – but was that as Christopher or Christine? Shit, this was getting far too complicated.

Driving home that evening, I was apprehensive about what I was going to find and how Sara would be with me.

Walking into the flat, I was hit by the aroma of a sauce on the stove. Sara put her head around the kitchen door.

"Hi Chris, I'm making a Spag Bol for dinner. Is that OK?"

"Fabulous. Have I got time to change?"

"Of course, I haven't put the spaghetti on yet and the sauce can simmer for a while. Do you want a glass of wine? I opened a bottle of red for the Bolognaise sauce."

"Let me shower first, I'll drink it while I get dressed and made up."

I was relieved that I hadn't been met at the door with a kiss or other show of affection – though a bit disappointed too if I was being honest.

As Sara sat down, she looked everywhere except at me.

"What is it," I asked.

She put down her fork and spoon, took a breath then said.

"About last night – and this morning. I put you in an awkward situation and I'm sorry. I'm also sorry if it might have given you the wrong impression."

"What do you mean?" I probed.

"That I want more than just friendship from you?"

"And you don't? You realise you've broken my heart, don't you?" I asked her.

She looked at me wide-eyed and lifted her hand to her mouth.

"I'm so sorry. I really am."

I smiled at her.

"Sara, you're a lovely lady and, yes, I could easily fancy you but I'd much rather keep you as a friend so eat your spaghetti, which is fabulous, by the way."

Chapter 23. Hot Cross Buns
Friday 10th April 1998

Sara went back to Inverness on the Friday having spent eleven days at the flat. Having cleared the air over our relationship, Sara pointed out that there was little point me using the sofa and I'd be much more comfortable sharing the bed – we'd just keep to our own sides.

Over the next couple of months, I usually returned home every other weekend and the project progressed according to plan with a few hiccups here and there – as usual with such work.

I continued to attend Northern Concord on Wednesday evenings and go down the Village on Friday and Saturday evenings if I wasn't at home and Sara and I chatted by phone at least once a week.

So, all in all, life became quite routine.

As Easter approached, I bought the largest chocolate egg I could find for Olivia and a box of Belgian chocolate liqueurs for Lucinda – which she'd probably complain about as being too fattening, though she'd still eat them.

I left work at lunchtime on the Thursday and headed south. Thankfully, most of the traffic was going the other way; making me wonder if there was anyone left in Birmingham or London.

At home, I emptied my suitcase of the bag of dirty laundry I'd brought back with me as the washing machine at the flat was playing up. I shook the contents into the machine, added soap powder and conditioner and set the machine to operate off-peak.

We had a late breakfast on Friday then attended the Good Friday church service. I felt a hypocrite as I no longer believed in what we were supposedly celebrating but Lucinda seemed to be getting more and more involved in St John's and it was easier to go along with her rather than get into a disagreement. I recognised one of the hymns from my childhood and added my voice to the rest of the congregation for 'There is a Green Hill Far Away'. If I thought attending the service on Good Friday meant we wouldn't be going on Easter Sunday, I was, sadly, mistaken. Lucinda was quite insistent that this was the most important time of the Christian year and we would attend as a family.

Saturday, however, was a free day. Olivia volunteered to help me clean my car – in exchange for a donation to her riding fund. It was a fair deal as the car was dirty outside and needed a thorough hoovering inside as well.

Lucinda had been sorting the laundry while I made some coffee for us and was about to put it in the washing machine when she saw that it was already full with my load from Thursday night.

"Why do you only ever do half a job?" she demanded to know as I filled a bucket with warm water to wash the car.

"Sorry, but I didn't think you wanted us to do any work like that on Good Friday and I forgot about it this morning," I replied. I grabbed a laundry basket from the corner of the utility room.

"Give it here," she commanded grabbing the basket. "You get on with the car."

As she pulled the clothes from the machine, she held up a pair of tights.

"What are these doing here?" she demanded to know. "How did they get mixed up with your stuff?"

Then she paused and looked more closely.

"Hang on a minute, these aren't mine. I use nude, these look like American Tan. So, whose are they?"

I realise I could be in the shit. But maybe there was a way out of it.

"Oh, they re mine," I said making it sound as matter-of-fact as I could.

"Since when did you start wearing t ghts?"

"Lots of the guys do on the site. It gets very cold and they keep us warm. If you remember, your dad wore a pair of your mums when we went to watch the motorcycle scrambl ng the winter before last," I told her.

"Oh yes," she admitted begrudgingly. "I thought for one moment you were having an affair – or you'd gone queer on me. You might find 60 deniers work a lot better though, these feel very lightweight."

I thanked my lucky stars for a close shave and resolved to take a lot more care with my things in future. Lucinda then re-loaded the machine and set it to wash while I removed the bucket of water from the sink and took it outside to the car.

Lucinda and I were having dinner with Dougie and Maureen that evening; the babysitter arrived at quarter to eight and, once Lucinda had briefed her, we donned our coats and walked up the road to the Edwards' house. Although it was dry, there was a bitter wind blowing and we pulled our coats even tighter. Maureen must have been watching out for us as we didn't even have to ring their bell before the front door opened.

"Come in out of the cold," she told us. "Here let me take your jackets."

Lucinda handed Maureen a bouquet we'd picked up from the florist in town.

"These are lovely, thanks very much, I'll pop them in a vase."

Dougie was standing behind his wife and, as she moved into the kitchen, he came forward and kissed Lucinda on the cheek then shook my hand. I gave him the bottle of wine we'd selected.

"Come on through to the lounge," he invited.

Their house was virtually the same layout as our own; part of a development of about fifty detached three and four-bedroom properties built about thirty years ago. Nearly all of the properties are owner-occupied, usually on substantial mortgages, forcing both partners to work in spite of the fact that most of them have young children. The original design included the double garage which ours retains. An increasing number of owners, including Dougie and Maureen, have converted one half of the garage into a study or playroom. As well as a door to the garage or study, stairs and a cloakroom, the hall leads to the kitchen located at the front of the house and through to the lounge at the rear.

Dougie stepped aside so we could go through to the lounge.

A welcoming log fire was blazing in the hearth, filling the room with the scent of pine.

"So, what would you like to drink Lucinda? Chris?" Dougie asked.

"G and T, please," Lucinda replied.

"Whiskey for you, Chris? I've a nice Jura single malt."

"Sounds perfect," I told him.

As he handed us our drinks, Maureen joined us and set the vase with the flowers on a side table. She then accepted the glass Dougie was offering her.

"Thanks, darling," she said. "Let's just have these aperitifs then I'll serve the starters."

Over dinner, Dougie dropped a bombshell.

"By the way, Chris. Lucinda tells me you're in Manchester the weekend of the 25th. There's a group of us going up for the match against Manchester City. We're booked into the Britannia Hotel near Piccadilly Gardens. We thought we'd go out for a meal afterwards. Maybe you'd like to join us One of the lads says China Town isn't far from the hotel."

The thought of joining a gang of football supporters after a match was close to the bottom of my list of 'things I'd like to do'.

"Unless, of course, you've got something else on?" he continued.

Lucinda had been about to eat a fork-load of salmon but she paused halfway between her plate and mouth and looked at me. Turning Douglas down might make her suspicious, especially after the tights incident.

"No, I haven't anything planned once I've supervised the work on-site in the afternoon, Chinese sounds good to me," I replied, smiling.

"Fine, do you have any recommendations?"

"Depends what you want, I like the Royal Peking, it's on Portland Street just outside China Town itself. They have an extensive buffet and is quite reasonable."

"That sounds perfect."

After the meal, after clearing the table, we returned to the lounge with our coffees and liqueurs. Dougie threw another log onto the fire – sending sparks flying up the chimney. He then took a pack of cards out of a drawer.

"Have you ever played 'Crazy Whist'" he asked.

"What's that?" Lucinda asked.

"It's sort of like Bridge but, as the name suggests, far less serious," Maureen said.

"We were introduced to this game a few years ago on a camping holiday with friends," Dougie remarked.

"The object is, like Bridge, to bid how many tricks you think you can take – then make your contract. But, instead of having fixed partners for the game, the highest bidder calls for a particular card from the other players and whoever has that card is their partner and that suit is trumps," Maureen explained.

"The other players also score the number of tricks they make so, they are both playing for themselves and as a partnership to stop the bidders making their contract," Dougie added.

"You'll get the hang of it quickly enough," Maureen assured us. "It's a lot of fun and best played with friends after a few drinks."

I knew Lucinda had played a lot of Bridge in the past but I'd never had the patience to learn the bidding conventions so she'd given up.

"Let's give it a go," Lucinda agreed.

Maureen proved to be right. It was a lot of fun. Dougie and I started to get into outrageous bidding wars almost regardless of what we had in our hands – counting on our partners having a decent hand if ours was rubbish. The further the level in the bottles of liqueurs fell, the wilder the bidding became. Lucinda and Maureen were a little more conservative and rarely failed to make their bids.

Dougie and I, on the other hand, sometimes bid ten or more tricks then failed to get them all. All too often, the most spectacular failures were when Dougie and I had both overbid on poor hands – then found ourselves in partnership with all the good cards in our opponents' hands.

As the clock on the mantlepiece approached midnight, Lucinda announced that we needed to make the current hand the last.

"We told the babysitter we'd be back about now," she remarked.

Chapter 24. Prawn Crackers
25th April 1998

The Britannia Hotel was right on the edge of the Gay Village – so I hoped and prayed that we wouldn't meet anyone who I knew while I was out with Dougie and his friends – or, if I did, that they were discrete. I drove around for several minutes trying to find a parking space that wasn't in one of the busiest parts of the Village and eventually found one on Minshull Street, around the corner from the hotel entrance.

We'd arranged to meet in the bar at seven-thirty – our table at the Royal Peking was booked for eight-thirty which gave us plenty of time. I knew Clive and Len from Dougie's barbecues but Wayne and Gary were new to me. It was clear that Wayne, in particular, had a head start as far as drinking was concerned. He was already slurring his words and I wondered if he'd be admitted to the restaurant. But maybe the walk in the fresh air would sober him up a bit. Well, I could hope.

The doorman at the Royal Peking did look askance at him but let us in and showed us to a table.

"So, Chris, what's the deal in here? Is it just serve yourself buffet?" Dougie asked.

"Yes, just grab a plate and help yourself – go back as often as you like, it's all you can eat. They'll probably kick us out after about an hour and a half," I told him. "You get drinks from the bar over there," I added, pointing it out.

"Are we doing a kitty for the drinks?" Len enquired.

"Can do, what shall we put in? Twenty each?" suggested Clive.

We each tossed our contribution onto the table. As I would be driving later, I knew I wouldn't get anything like my fair share of the drinks but commenting would make me look like a wimp and I had to keep up the appearance of being one of the boys.

Dougie took control of the kitty and the two of us went to get six pints of lager from the bar while the others joined the short queue for the buffet. Having deposited the drinks on the table, we joined the queue ourselves.

Bob's plate was piled high – I doubted if he could fit another prawn anywhere; which probably explained his girth. He had a crewcut and various tattoos on his arms and neck. I wouldn't fancy taking him on in a fight. Wayne was the other extreme, but wiry rather than skinny – the muscles he did have looked hardened. Like Bob, he was tattooed. And, again, he wasn't someone I'd want to tangle with. But then, I prefer to avoid physical conflict if at all possible.

"So, Chris, what's your line of business?" Bob asked. "And, what keeps you in Manchester at the weekend? Dougie's been hinting at nefarious goings on. Got a bit on the side up here, have you?" he guffawed. He nudged Wayne causing him to spill some of the beer he was about to drink.

"Watch it, you clumsy oaf. For Christ's sake," Wayne complained.

"Sorry mate, plenty more where that came from," Bob responded.

"Fuck me, what's that coming through the door?" Wayne exclaimed.

I looked and recognised Gina and Michelle from the Village. I suspected they were getting a meal before starting work. Both wore mini-skirts, tight low-cut tops and boots with three-inch stiletto heels; all designed to sell what they were offering. Gina wore a platinum blond wig while Michelle's was red. They made no attempt to blend in – and why should they?

The doorman was looking at his watch and seemed to be indicating, apologetically, quite a wait before they could be given a table. He pointed to the bar, possibly suggesting they have a drink while they waited but after a brief consultation, they seemed to decide not to stay. They weren't particular friends of mine though I'd spoken to them a few times and I doubted that they'd recognise me in drab. But it was still a shock seeing them there.

"God, what a sight. Have you ever seen anything like it? I thought Lilly Savage had walked in," Wayne said.

"Well, if you don't want to see lots more like that, then don't wander off to the right of Portland Street," I told them. "The area's known as the Gay Village and all the clubs are for gay men and women and transgender people."

"And how do you know about it? Chris? Personal experience?" Len demanded to know, chortling.

"Everyone in Manchester knows about the Gay Village," I remarked as casually as I could, before picking up another piece of barbecued rib.

The conversation then turned to the football match which had, apparently, ended in a two-all draw. I got lost when they started discussing individual players' performances – I didn't even know who played for whom. Nor did I care.

"Not a football fan then?" asked Wayne.

"Sorry, no. I prefer rugby, but each to their own."

"How can you not appreciate the beautiful game?" he demanded. "It's key to our heritage. Have you never been to a match?"

"I've been to three," I told him. "I was dragged along twice to games with an uncle and a cousin and once to an international at Wembley as the guest of a supplier who invited me and my boss at the time. We went on to a Greek restaurant afterwards which I did enjoy."

"So, who was the match against? What was the final score?"

"I think it was Poland but I've no idea of the score. I think England won though."

The others were watching me as though I'd sprouted two heads. I don't think they'd have been more surprised if I'd been dressed like Gina and Michelle.

 Bob made three more trips to the buffet for main courses before declaring himself ready for his pudding. The others had refilled their plates twice; I'd been back to the buffet once but made sure that I didn't have too much each time. There was a dress I'd seen that I wanted but I needed to drop a size before I could get in it.

As we left the restaurant, Bob belched then lit a cigarette before draping his arm around my shoulder.

"That was a good feed," he mumbled. "Bloody good choice of restaurant. Now we need to get some serious drinking in."

We stopped at the junction with Princess Street for the lights to change so we could cross.

"Hang on a minute," Clive called. "If this is Princess Street, is there a Whitworth Street near here? A mate at work told me about an Irish pub on the corner of those streets. Should get a decent pint of Guinness there."

"Probably means O'Shea's. It's a couple of hundred yards down there," I said pointing down the road.

"That's the one. Right guys follow me," he said.

A drizzle had started to fall – for which I was grateful as we walked past the New Union bar on the corner of Canal Street; it kept most of the customers inside rather than spilling onto the paved area beside the canal.

Traditional Irish music was playing as we entered the pub. Dougie, as holder of the kitty, went to the bar with Clive while the rest of us found space to stand and listen to the band. Seeing that I'd switched to Coke as I'd be driving later, Dougie handed me the rest of the kitty as he wasn't sure any of the others would be in any fit state by the end of the evening.

It had gone midnight by the time we left O'Shea's and started to walk back up Princess Street. The earlier drizzle had stopped and it had turned into a pleasant evening – bringing revellers out of the New Union and onto the pedestrianised area by the Rochdale Canal. As we approached, Bob pointed out some of the 'sights'.

"Fuck me, there's more of those trannies like the ones we saw in the restaurant. Mind you some of those actually look quite tasty," he remarked in a voice made louder by the amount he'd drunk during the evening.

"I think we'll have a bit of fun with the pansies," he said. "Come on."

He started to cross the road for a closer look followed by Wayne, Len, Clive and Dougie. I brought up the rear trying to stay as inconspicuous as I could as I recognised a couple of the girls. If I hadn't been out on this 'boys' night', I'd probably have been with them.

"Are those tits real? *Darling'* Bob asked one of the two girls leaning against the wall by the canal – pointing to her cleavage.

She ignored him and continued chatting to her friend.

"Hey. I asked you a question? It's not polite ignoring me. So, do you take it up the bum then?"

She gave him a withering look then just said "Piss off."

"That's not very friendly, now, is it? No, come on, I want to know. Or are you a Lessie?" he turned to Wayne.

"What do you think, mate? Do you reckon she sucks or fucks or is she a dyke?"

Len, Clive and Dougie held back, staying on the pavement, distancing themselves from the scene. I couldn't, however, just stand by and ignore what was going on. I walked over and took hold of Bob's arm.

"Come on Bob, you're out of order. They're just minding their own business and not doing anyone any harm. Leave them alone."

Bob looked at me – then over my shoulder.

"What's the problem here?" a deep voice asked from well above my shoulder height. I turned round to find myself staring into the chest of one of the doormen from the New Union.

"That dickhead and his mate, there, were having a go at us, Cliff. This bloke seems to be with them but was trying to get them to stop," said the target of Bob's abuse.

"Right, gents. I suggest that if you don't like what you see around here, you fuck off out of the Gay Village," said Cliff as he marshalled Bob and Wayne back onto Princess Street – then gave them a gentle push along the road.

Zoë was looking at me curiously.

"I don't recognise your face, but your voice sounds familiar," she said.

"Well, I've shared the dance floor with you often enough in Naps, Zoë, and you Wendy" I replied quietly.

"Chris," Wendy exclaimed. "What the fuck was the idea of bringing those wankers to the Village."

"Shush, please. One of the guys I'm with is a neighbour from home he doesn't know anything about me. So, keep it schtum, please," I begged. "I tried to keep them away from the Village but we'd been to O'Shea's and there wasn't any other way back to their hotel. They're friends of a friend. Here, get yourselves a drink on them," I said; giving the girls twenty pounds from the kitty.

Zoë winked, "Your secret's safe with us. Come on Wendy, let's spend that wanker's money, what do you fancy?"

I walked back to where Dougie, Len and Clive were waiting on the bridge over the canal.

"You seemed to know those trannies, you spent a while talking to them," Dougie remarked.

"How would I know them? I was just apologising for Bob's behaviour. He was well out of order. Living in Manchester, you learn to respect the

Gay Village even if you aren't part of the scene or don't necessarily agree with what goes on. So, I gave them twenty from the kitty to get themselves a drink. That can come out of what's left of Bob and Wayne's shares. Any objections?"

"No, seems fair to me," Dougie replied.

I turned to the others. "Len? Clive?"

"Fine by me," said Len

"And me," echoed Clive.

I hoped I'd got away without causing too much suspicion – but the sideways looks I had from Dougie were worrying.

Chapter 25. Barbecue
May 1998

We spent the end of May bank holiday at home. On the Saturday evening, it was our turn to entertain Maureen and Dougie. On Saturday morning I dragged the barbecue out of the shed and cleaned off the debris that had gathered over the winter. We'd run out of charcoal and lighter fuel so I drove to a nearby garage and stocked up.

The sun was blazing in a clear blue sky with just the faintest of breezes rustling the upper branches of the apple and pear trees in the garden; I ran the mower over the lawn then set up a gazebo and put a picnic table inside it. It made a change to be able to relax in the garden with the sound of birds in the hedges and taller trees; bees were buzzing and butterflies were flitting amongst the flowers.

Overhead I could see the vapour trails from airliners way above us – flying from Stansted or Birmingham, or, possibly, Manchester to European destinations or places even further afield. As I sat back in my chair, I became aware of the hum of aero engines getting closer. I shaded my eyes and searched the sky for the source of the sound. Then I saw three dots that gradually expanded until I could recognise the RAF's Battle of Britain Memorial Flight of Hurricane and Spitfire fighters and the four-engine Lancaster bomber. They weren't an unusual sight for us as they used a large reservoir nearby as a checkpoint for their flights to air displays. Nevertheless, they were always a reminder of my younger days plane spotting and attending air displays and of a dream of being a pilot in the RAF myself. Perhaps if that dream had come true, it would have distracted me from my transgender feelings. The sound of the six Merlin engines grew louder as they approached, passing no more than half a mile from where we were.

About half an hour before we expected our friends, I lit the barbecue then brought out the drinks – storing bottles of white wine and beer, together with some fruit juice for the girls, in a storage crate part filled with water and ice to keep them well chilled.

When our friends arrived, Lucinda brought out the salads and laid them on the table. I poured Maureen and Lucinda a glass of wine each, handed Dougie a beer and took one for myself. After her first sip, Lucinda put her glass down and went into the kitchen to bring out the meat, which had been marinating, for the barbecue. The coals were glowing white hot by now so I started to spread the meat on the grill.

As the steaks reached the stage that each person wanted, I served them onto their plates and they added salads. The girls put burgers or sausages between sliced rolls and sat on a blanket on the grass to eat theirs accompanied by glasses of fruit juice. Lucinda had made a fresh fruit salad to follow served with fresh cream or ice cream.

Once they'd finished eating, Olivia dragged June off to the bottom of the garden to play with her rabbits and guinea pig leaving the adults to chat. I refilled Maureen and Lucinda's glasses, poured one for myself and passed Dougie another beer.

"I had words with Wayne and Bob after that trouble in Manchester, I told them I agreed with you that they'd been out of order," Dougie told me.

"What trouble was that?" Lucinda asked.

"When we met up with Chris after the match in Manchester last month, we went out for a meal. On the way back to the hotel, Wayne and Bob, mainly Bob, spotted some trannies outside a pub in the Gay Village and started to take the piss," Dougie replied.

"Language, darling," Maureen chastised.

"Trannies and Gay Village. What were you doing in places like that?" Lucinda demanded.

"We'd been to an Irish pub which happened to be just outside the Village. The road back to the hotel they were staying at is the boundary of the Gay area in Manchester. We didn't actually go in the area; well not initially," I explained.

"So, what happened?" she insisted.

"As I said, Bob and Wayne started to abuse two transvestites but Chris asked them to stop," Dougie said.

"But why did you interfere, Chris?" she asked.

"The transvestites were minding their own business and didn't deserve the abuse. I just tried to defuse the situation and get Bob and Wayne away from there," I told her.

"Well, to be honest, I'm not sure that I don't agree with Bob and Wayne telling them off. I certainly hope you aren't mixing with such disgusting people," Lucinda said as she stood up and walked back into the house.

I was relieved that she'd cut off any further discussion but any doubts I might have had about how she'd react if she ever learned that I was also trans had been eliminated. I would have to take very great care to make sure that never happened.

She returned a few minutes later with a cheeseboard and crackers which she put out on the table. I cut myself a wedge of Double Gloucester and buttered some Cornish Wafers.

"Lovely cheeses, Lucinda, where did you buy them?" Maureen asked.

"The deli counter in Waitrose," Lucinda replied.

As the sun set, Maureen announced that they needed to get June home to bed, though it was another twenty minutes before they actually left and Lucinda and I were able to clear up the remnants of the party and load the crockery into the dishwasher.

The next morning, Olivia and I were required to accompany Lucinda to St John's. The sermon focussed on the importance of maintaining traditional family values and not straying from the teachings of the Bible. The minister reminded those present of what happened to Sodom and Gomorrah when the inhabitants ignored God's will. After the service, we stayed, again at Lucinda's insistence, for coffee with other members of the congregation. Olivia wandered off to talk to one of her school friends. Lucinda's church friends praised the sermon and decried campaigns for women priests and the idea that homosexuals should be allowed to marry.

"Those deviants are even campaigning to be able to spread their perversions amongst school children, would you believe? No doubt to try to recruit them. They want to overturn Margaret Thatcher's ban on spreading their evil," said one, glancing around to ensure this unsavoury topic wasn't overheard by any children.

"The trouble is that this socialist government might just give in to them," said another – with considerable bile on the word 'socialist'.

I tried to remain silent to avoid raising more questions in Lucinda's mind but it wasn't to be.

"What do you think, Christopher?" asked one.

I thought for a moment before answering.

"Isn't what people do in private entirely their business?"

I wanted to say a lot more but didn't dare to.

"Yes, well, that's all very well, but the Bible is quite clear on the subject," she replied before turning away to talk to the minister.

As we left the church, it seemed to me that Lucinda's and the minister's handshake was held a fraction longer than when he wished others goodbye. But perhaps I imagined it.

Chapter 26. Frying Pan or Fire?
June 1998

On the drive back to Manchester on Monday afternoon, I pondered the way the weekend had gone. I hoped the issue of my defence of Zoë and Wendy had been dropped and that my explanations, such as they were, had been accepted. If not, I could be in trouble, serious trouble.

Lucinda hadn't mentioned the matter again over the rest of the bank holiday weekend so I tried to continue as normal. I hadn't mentioned the way she and the minister had held each other's hands after coffee on Sunday either. I couldn't help wondering if something was going on between them.

Would I care if there was? Yes, I would. Not because of any impact on Lucinda or me, but because it would affect Olivia. If I was honest with myself, I couldn't see our marriage surviving in the long term – and I wasn't sure I particularly cared. I didn't, however, want to interrupt Olivia's schooling. She was due to sit her GCSEs next year and her A levels two years later.

Of course, if Lucinda ever found out about my cross-dressing, the matter might be taken out of my hands. Not that it stopped me getting changed as soon as I got back to the flat or attending Northern Concord on Wednesdays – and heading to Napoleons later in the evening for a dance. Inevitably, I bumped into Zoë and Wendy on one of those trips in the upstairs bar at Naps.

"Who the hell were those dickheads who had a go at us outside the New Union?" Zoë demanded.

"They were friends of one of my neighbours from home; well, I'm not even sure he'd describe them as friends. They'd come to watch their team play City and Dougie, that's my neighbour, invited me to join them for a meal. I couldn't refuse without raising suspicions about what I got up to on a Saturday evening when I stayed in Manchester," I explained.

"Fine, but why bring them into the Village?"

"I didn't. We had a meal at the Royal Peking then they wanted to go to O'Shea's for a drink. They were stopping at the Britannia so the only way to their hotel was past the New Union. They'd seen Michelle and Gina earlier in the restaurant and when Bob and Wayne saw you two, they decided to take the piss. I'm so sorry it happened."

"Yeah, well, wasn't your fault I suppose and you did slip us the twenty pounds," Zoë conceded. "Come on Wendy, let's dance."

Arriving home that evening, I noticed a rather beaten-up Vauxhall Cavalier across the road from the flat. There seemed to be one male sitting in it. I couldn't see him clearly as he was parked midway between lampposts. I turned into the drive leading to the parking area behind the flats, parked up and walked down the side path to my door. Without switching on the light, I went into the lounge and looked out but couldn't see the car clearly as there was a hedge in the way.

I wondered if it might be a drug dealer. I'd heard they often used old cars that wouldn't be missed if they were confiscated. I put it out of my mind as I got undressed and cleansed and toned my face.

The car was there again when I got back from work the next evening. This time, it was still light so I could see that the occupant was a white male probably mid-forties, clean-shaven with shortish salt and pepper hair. As I drove past him, he turned his head away and seemed to be looking at something on the seat next to him.

When I saw him again the next night, I started to get annoyed. I stopped next to him and was winding my window down when he started his engine and drove off.

Why had he been there? He didn't look like my idea of a drug dealer – but, then, I didn't know any dealers as far as I was aware. And, would he have just driven off? Surely he'd have an explanation for casual enquiries about his behaviour.

As it was a Friday, I got changed, had dinner and drove into the Village. The guy in the car had gone.

Arriving home the following Friday, I was surprised to find Lucinda on her own and no sign of Olivia.

"Olivia's staying with June tonight," Lucinda told me as I dropped my case in the hall.

"So, who is she?" she demanded, handing me some photographs taken from inside the front garden at the flat. They showed me standing in the lounge smoking. I realised that the man I'd seen round the flat had been a private investigator.

"And, what's she doing driving your car?" she added, handing me more photographs showing me driving out of the drive.

I had to think quickly. Lucinda hadn't realised the photographs were of me and obviously thought I was having an affair. Knowing her opinion of cross-dressers, the truth wasn't going to help. In fact, it would make matters much worse.

"That's Elizabeth from the office. I needed her to collect one of the directors who was flying in from Brussels that evening from the airport and take him to his hotel. Her car wasn't suitable so I lent her mine for the evening," I explained.

"And, why couldn't he just get a taxi?"

"He needed some papers to go over ready for a meeting the next morning. Liz was taking them with her when she collected him."

"So, if I call this Elizabeth, she'll confirm your story?"

"Of course, she will."

"So, what's her number?"

"I don't have it, she had mine to call me if there were any problems."

She stared at me, her eyebrows furrowed.

"Do you expect me to believe this story?"

"It's the truth. You surely don't think I'm having an affair, do you? For goodness sake, if I was having an affair with Liz, why wouldn't I be in the car with her?"

I could see that had stopped her in her tracks.

"Look, give her a call at the office on Monday if you don't believe me."

If Lucinda called my bluff, I'd have to persuade Liz to back me up – or have someone tell Lucinda that Liz was off sick or on leave or something. I could organise that on Monday morning.

"What on earth made you hire someone to spy on me in any case?"

"I found this in the car last time you were home." She held up an earring. "That, plus the tights, started me wondering – especially as you've changed since working up there. You used to believe the same as me and wouldn't have defended trannies before."

"Several of the others use my car if they need it; it's not my personal property and making it available to other staff reduces the tax bill. I assume one of the girls dropped the earring. Where did you find it?"

"On the driver's side; by the door."

"Well, there you go. It would've been when one of the staff used the car. Maybe it got caught on the seat belt. If I'd been taking a girl out in the car, surely it would have been on the passenger side. Can you imagine me letting someone else drive me?"

"I don't know. But if I find out you have been having an affair, you'll regret it."

Chapter 27. Bubbly
July 1998

I first encountered Elizabeth in the Village one Saturday evening earlier in the year when she'd been out with her girlfriend. I'd gone into Paddy's Goose and the only spare seats had been at their table.

"Come and join us," she'd invited.

"I'm Elizabeth, this is Kirsty, is this one of your regular haunts?" she asked.

"Yes, I'm in here most Wednesdays and Saturdays when I'm in Manchester. I'm Chris, by the way," I said.

We got chatting and they told me that they'd moved to Manchester because Kirsty had started a new job at one of the central hospitals. Elizabeth was going to register for temp work with agencies while she looked round for a permanent position.

Three weeks later, she'd turned up at our office in response to a request I'd made for extra staff. She didn't recognise me immediately but, as I explained the work I needed her to do, she began to glance questioningly at me.

"Have we met before, Chris?" she eventually asked. Then her eyes opened wide for a moment and I knew she'd remembered.

"In Paddy's Goose, you were there with Kirsty," I said quietly, thankful that my office door was closed and none of the other staff could overhear.

"Of course. I take it no one here knows of your alter ego. Don't worry, your secret is safe with me. The agency doesn't know about me either. It's none of their business"

She'd proved very capable, I'd encouraged her to take on more of the project management tasks and I'd been able to persuade Ed, my boss, to take her on permanently. I'd been round to their flat for dinner a couple of times and they knew about my family background and the fact that Lucinda knew nothing of Christine.

When I got to the office on Tuesday morning, Liz was at her desk in the outer office.

"Can you spare me a minute please, Liz," I asked.

She picked up her notebook and followed me. I took off my jacket and hung it up.

"What's the problem, Chris?"

"Lucinda has had me followed and she has photographs of a woman driving my car and standing in my lounge. I'm sorry, but I told her that it was you. It was the only thing I could think of on the spur of the moment."

"And you want me to confirm your story? Wouldn't it be easier to just tell her the truth?" She paused for a moment then shook her head. "No, you're right, from what you've told me about her attitude. But you know it'll come out sometime, don't you?"

"Maybe, but not until Olivia has finished her GSCEs and A levels. I really don't want to interrupt those. After that, I don't care if Lucinda and I *do* split up."

"Well, Chris, she sure as hell isn't going to stay with you when you decide to transition – and don't tell me you haven't thought about that."

"I've no intention of transitioning – I'm very happy cross-dressing. Far too many problems going any further; it would cost me everything, not just Olivia but my job, the house, any prospects for the future. That's not for me."

 Her look told me what she thought of my reply.

"Whatever. Back to the immediate problem – what's the story I have to give your wife?"

I told Liz the tale I'd fed Lucinda.

"OK, I'll back you up. But keep in mind what I said. Sooner or later..."

I was passing Liz's desk later that morning when I overheard her side of a phone call.

"Yes, that's right Mrs Williamson. Mr Williamson asked me to print off some papers for the next day's meeting then take copies to him, collect his car from his flat, collect Herr Werner from the airport and take him to his hotel."

I could hear Lucinda replying but couldn't make out her words.

"Yes, Mrs Williamson, I had to give Herr Werner copies of the papers as well. An inconvenience? Not at all; I was glad of the overtime, to be honest. It was my partner's and my anniversary and I was able to treat us to a bottle of Champagne."

Liz fell silent, listening to Lucinda again.

"No, Mrs Williamson, your husband doesn't take advantage of us. He's a very considerate boss. It's a pleasure to work for him. Oh, and I gather you found my sapphire earring – that's such a relief. I thought I'd lost it and they were a present."

"No problem, Mrs Williamson. Goodbye," Liz said as she ended the call.

"OK?" she asked me.

"Thanks very much, Liz, I take it she was convinced?"

"I think so. Unless she's a better actress than me."

"I owe you and Kirsty a bottle of bubbly," I told her.

"Well, we have to stick together, don't we? But a bottle of fizz would be nice."

That week passed quickly as we were preparing progress reports for a meeting at Head Office on Friday. Liz was a whiz at laying out the data on PowerPoint and rehearsing the presentation with me.

Fortunately, the meeting went well. There were some parts of the project that were behind schedule due to unforeseen problems but, overall, we were only a few weeks late and well within the contingency budget. I sighed with relief when the Chairman turned to the rest of the board of directors when the questions seemed to have dried up.

"Any other points on the relocation? No? Then thank you Williamson. Good work."

A quick smile in my direction then he turned to the next set of papers in front of him.

"Yes, excellent work, Chris," said Ed as we left the boardroom, "You were clearly the right choice for the job. I need a chat with you, come along to my office."

I didn't think I was in trouble; well, not after having been thanked for my efforts by the Chairman, but the project was now in its final phase and I'd been wondering what would happen to me afterwards. I was reasonably confident that I'd still have a job – though companies like ours could be ruthless.

Once the relocation programme was completed, there'd be no need for me to be in Manchester unless I was transferred there permanently; either way, I'd lose the allowances that paid for the flat. Could we afford the flat without the allowances? Not without cutting back significantly. I was quite certain that Lucinda and Olivia wouldn't want to move to Manchester so where would that leave me?

As we reached Ed's office, he turned to his secretary, asked her if there were any messages then if she'd make us some coffee.

"Take a seat, Chris. You've probably been wondering what happens once Manchester is complete?"

"I certainly have," I told him.

"The MD was very impressed with the way you managed the project and wants you to retain overall responsibility for the site as you are so familiar with it. It's a promotion for you. The board has also decided to establish distribution centres in the Northeast and Scotland and you'll be handling those projects."

"So, where would I be based? And is there a pay rise involved?"

"Yes, there is an increase in salary, it's around nine thousand. As for location, you could transfer to Manchester. Property is much cheaper there than in Cambridgeshire, you'd be able to afford a larger place if you wanted; I suspect that might appeal to Lucinda."

"It might, but I know she doesn't want to move and I don't think it would be fair on Olivia especially as she's taking her GCSE's next year. I don't think she'd want to leave her friends either."

"Yes, I suspected as much. I feel the same way, my wife doesn't want to move either — several others in the senior management group are in the same position. We've persuaded the board to retain a strategic corporate office here," Ed said. "You could remain officially based here but, as you already receive an allowance for working away from home, you wouldn't be able to claim extra for trips to the other sites."

The pay rise even after tax and other deductions, would cover bed and breakfast costs if I needed to stop over in the northeast or Scotland and most of the time I could probably drive there and back in a day.

"Sounds great, Ed, thanks for the confidence."

"No problem, Chris, you've earned it."

"Now get off home and discuss the offer with Lucinda."

Outside, I put my briefcase in the luggage compartment of my car, hung my jacket up on the hook behind my seat then slid behind the wheel. Instead of my usual three-hour drive home on a Friday, it should only take about an hour from Head Office.

The M1 traffic was building up with the exodus from London but, with no incidents or roadworks, I was at the turn-off less than 30 minutes later. A few miles further on, I passed the lane down which I'd stopped to get changed eighteen months ago and had been spoken to by the police patrol. Thankfully, I didn't need to take that sort of risk any longer.

Olivia was chatting to her friend June when I pulled onto the drive.

"DAD!" she yelled, rushing to grab me as I got out of the car. I held her to me and gave her a kiss. In that moment, I thought, not for the first time, about the risks I was still taking with our lives. Maybe I needed to try once more to stop 'dressing'. Maybe I needed to decide what was truly important for me.

Lucinda was in the lounge with Reverend Parker.

"Howard was explaining that St John's church hall needs to be renovated and they're looking for somewhere to hold the weekly bible reading group in the meantime. I said he could hold it here. I take it that's OK with you," she said.

"Yes, fine. I'm not here in any case so it doesn't affect me."

"Very kind of you, Christopher. It's a great pity you're unable to join us but I gather you're away during the week. Manchester, isn't it? I don't know how you can work in a place that celebrates sinful behaviour," he said, fingering his dog collar.

I wasn't going to get into an argument with him so I just stood there.

"Yes, well, I must be off," he said. "God's work to be done, you know. I'll see you on Sunday Lucinda."

Lucinda glared at me. "Certainly, Howard, I'll see you out."

I walked into the kitchen, and put the bottle of Champagne I'd bought on the way home in the fridge to cool. The kettle already had water in it so I switched it on.

"Did you have to be so rude?" she asked as she joined me.

"What did I say?" I asked; adding instant coffee to a couple of mugs.

"Oh, never mind, what's the point?" she said in exasperation as she opened the fridge door for the milk.

"What's this doing here?" she asked holding up the bubbly.

"I thought we'd celebrate this evening."

"Celebrate what?"

"I've been promoted. I'm now responsible for the Manchester site and two more projects."

"I hope that doesn't mean we have to move up there. Because you can forget that for a start."

"No, the package means I officially remain based at Head Office but spend most of my time in Manchester or the other sites."

"So, how much is the pay rise?"

As usual, Lucinda was probably already spending the extra in her mind.

Chapter 28. Stargazy Pie
7th August 1998

The following weekend, I managed to get away early and, as traffic was lighter than normal, I arrived home more than an hour before usual. Lucinda was in the dining room with Reverend Howard Parker and two other church members, sitting at the table with various sheets of flip chart paper spread around. She stood up and came into the kitchen.

"I wasn't expecting you until later. Sorry, we're having a meeting," she said as I kissed her on the cheek. "We'll be finished shortly." Parker started to tidy the sheets into a pile but I got a glimpse of one which had 'Repent, homosexuality is a sin!' written in bold block capitals, before he covered it with other sheets showing only their blank sides.

"What's going on?" I asked.

"I'll tell you later," she responded as she closed the dining room door behind her. I picked up the kettle to make myself a cup of coffee, wondering where Olivia was – probably out with her friend June.

"I think we're finished for today, in any case," I heard Parker say. "I'll bring the actual placards and paint on Wednesday – if that's still OK, Lucinda?"

"Absolutely, Howard. We'll paint them in the garage," my wife replied.

I then heard the doors between the dining room and lounge and from the lounge into the hall opening as they left. There was no way Lucinda would allow them through the kitchen, obviously.

I watched through the kitchen window as Mrs Gray and Miss Bennett left through the front door. There was a pause of at least two to three minutes before Reverend Parker then followed. No doubt he and Lucinda were just having a few final words.

When Lucinda joined me in the kitchen, I pointed to the kettle.

"Do you want a coffee? The water's just boiled," I asked.

"No, I'm fine. I made a pot for the committee."

"So, are you going to tell me what's going on?" I enquired.

"Howard believes that it's not enough to just worship God ourselves, we need to spread his word – just as St John, himself, did. He's raised funding for us to take the word to the sinners in Manchester when they hold their Mardi Gras parade over August Bank Holiday. We are going to join other Christians and display placards outside the Town Hall as the parade goes past."

I was stunned.

"It was your incident that made me suggest Manchester for our demonstration. It's a den of iniquity."

I didn't know what to say. I hadn't planned to be in the parade but I knew several friends would be – not that I thought the demonstration would have any impact. I suspected they'd just be regarded as harmless idiots. But, did Lucinda plan to use the flat? If she did, that would be a problem. I'd need to defeminise it thoroughly and store all my female items elsewhere for the time being.

Did she expect me to take part? What about Olivia?

"You're not planning to take Olivia with you, are you?" I asked.

"No, I assumed you'd be home that weekend; you hadn't said you'd be away. So, you can look after her. We plan to travel up on Friday and come back after church service on Sunday. We gather the parade is on the Saturday."

"OK, yes, that's fine," I said, relieved that it didn't sound like she planned to use the flat.

"Where are you staying in Manchester?" I asked.

"We're not. We're being hosted by a church in Liverpool; the congregation has offered to put us up. Our hosts are joining us on the protest."

I wanted to say that I didn't agree with their plans, but that risked being asked why I would defend the 'sinners'. So, I kept quiet even though I felt like a Judas.

"I hope you're not going to be in any danger, demonstrating. You don't want to get into trouble with the police," I told her.

"Why would we get into trouble with the police? We are law-abiding Christians defending our faith. In any case, God will protect us. We're doing his work."

I wasn't going to win any argument, so I left it at that.

"OK. Do what you think you must," I said. "I'll see if Olivia and June want to visit Woburn Safari Park on the Saturday or Sunday."

At that moment, Olivia and June came in through the kitchen door with Max and Maya, our two Pugs. The dogs tried to jump up at me as Olivia gave me a hug.

"Girls, would you like to go to the safari park over the August bank holiday?" I asked.

"Which day?" June asked. "I think Mum and Dad were planning to ask if 'Liv wanted to come with us to Ferry Meadows to go on the steam train on one of the days."

"It doesn't matter which day. Maybe they can take you there on one of the days and I'll take you to Woburn on the other. In fact, I might join you at Ferry Meadows as well."

"That would be brilliant, Dad," Olivia enthused. "What about Mum?"

"I'm going on a trip with the church so will be away until Sunday evening, darling," Lucinda replied.

"Oh, OK. Would have been nice to be together as a family," Olivia said.

"We can go out somewhere on the Monday, Olivia. I'm sure Dad can wait until Tuesday morning to travel back to Manchester — even if it means having to leave early."

"Absolutely," I answered. "Perhaps we can have a cycle ride around the reservoir. Maybe take a picnic with us."

Lucinda had already returned home from Manchester on Sunday when we got back from the safari park. She seemed to be rather dejected.

"How did it go?" I asked.

"We were jeered and laughed at," she said. "Everyone up there seemed to support the gays and turn their backs on Christ. It's as bad as Sodom and Gomorrah. No good will come of it, mark my words. Even the police seemed to be more interested in protecting the parade than stopping spectators from being nasty to us – some even sprayed us with big water pistols but the police did nothing. It's an awful place, I don't know how you stand working up there."

When I arrived in Manchester on Tuesday morning, I got down to work. Liz told me she'd been on a float in the Mardi Gras parade and showed me photographs of the floats and the crowds lining the route as it wound around the city centre. She even had some of the protesters outside the town hall.

I pointed to a figure holding a banner reading 'God Hates Gays'.

"That's Lucinda," I told her.

"Oh, God. I sprayed the man next to her with my water cannon."

"That's Reverend Parker. I hope you got him fair and square. I don't have any time for his hypocrisy."

"I sure did. A policeman nearby saw me and waggled his finger at me. Mind you, he was trying very hard not to laugh."

"I wish I could have been with you on the parade. It looks fabulous."

"Maybe next time."

Chapter 29. Battered Ribs
September 1998

I should have taken the warning from the attack on Sara and the abuse that Bob and Wayne had given Zoë and Wendy – but I never thought it would happen to me. But, it did. It wasn't even in the Village but when I was shopping at the supermarket one evening. I was putting the bags into my car when I was pushed against the open boot by a shove in the back.

"Fucking tranny," a voice said as a punch hit me in the kidneys.

"Your sort aren't wanted round here," said a second voice. Then something hit me on the back of the head causing me to see stars, literally.

I called for help. But there didn't seem to be anyone around. Well, no one who was prepared to come to my assistance.

Then a hand gripped my arm and pulled me round to face my attackers. The next punch hit me on the side of my head, then I took one to the stomach; making me double over. I could see three pairs of legs. Two of the owners were holding me from either side while the third person pummelled me.

"Oi! Leave her alone," I heard shouted from the entrance to the store.

The punches paused, then the two hands holding me let go and I dropped to the ground. Each of the attackers then kicked me before running away; taking my handbag with them.

"Are you OK, love?" asked my rescuer, one of the store's security staff.

"I think so," I told her.

"Let's get you back into the store and sort you out. Are you OK walking? Here, take my arm."

She helped me into the shop and into an office – probably one they used to interview shoplifters.

"You're going to have a few cuts and bruises and a black eye, but I don't think there's anything broken. You might well have concussion from the blow to the head and that's bleeding a bit so you might need a couple of stitches. You'd best go to A&E for a check-up just in case there's more to the head wound than I think. I've called for an ambulance for you," she told me.

I really didn't want to go to the hospital – there could be too many questions and consequences, but my head was throbbing and I could feel the blood on my scalp.

The ambulance arrived about forty-five minutes later, but it was another hour in A&E before I was seen by a doctor. An x-ray confirmed that my skull wasn't fractured but when I told him that I lived on my own, he was reluctant to release me.

"You really ought to have someone with you for the first twenty-four hours," he advised.

The only people I could ask to help out were Liz and Kirsty. Fortunately, they insisted that I stay at their flat overnight and drove over to pick me up.

Thankfully, there were no side effects from the concussion but my face was a mess and I had various other bruises so even moving around was painful. A more immediate problem was that I only had female clothes with me and they were in a mess and my car was still at the supermarket At least, I hoped it was.

It was. But it had been vandalised. 'Tranny' had been scratched into the paintwork along both sides.

Getting in the car was uncomfortable; Liz's was a 'sit up and beg' style so the seats were relatively high – minimising the need to bend over. Mine was much lower-slung. Eventually, I managed to get into the seat and start the car. Fortunately, while loading the car, I'd slipped the keys into the pocket of my jacket rather than putting them in my handbag.

By the time I got to the flat, my head was banging again and different bruises were competing for attention. Liz had gone on to the office after dropping me at my car so I phoned her.

"Can you let everyone know I'm off sick today – that I was mugged but I'll be back in tomorrow with luck."

"I thought you weren't supposed to be on your own for twenty-four hours," she pointed out. "Shall I come over? I could work on the report on the laptop."

I wasn't convinced it was necessary but didn't feel up to arguing.

After speaking to her, I called the insurance company and explained about the damage to the car. I really didn't want to drive around in it with 'tranny' on the sides; I certainly didn't want to take it home in that state. They said it would be picked up the following day and agreed to provide a hire car while mine was being repaired. I suppose I should have reported the attack to the police, too. But I really didn't want to have the fact that I was trans recorded on their database.

I didn't tell Lucinda about the attack either, because I didn't want her or Olivia worrying. I hadn't been due to go home the following weekend in any case and hoped the bruising would disappear over the next ten days.

I thought I'd covered all the bases.

Chapter 30. Goose Cooked?
September 1998

The car was returned a week later with no trace of any damage. The bruises had faded and the black eye and other cuts had healed. I didn't think I'd need to refer to the incident at home.

As usual, I picked up fish and chips for our dinner, expecting Lucinda and Olivia to be ready with the table laid and the plates warmed up. Olivia wasn't around though.

Lucinda seemed distant when I gave her a quick peck on the cheek and handed her the food. She put it to one side and handed me a letter.

"Care to explain this?" she asked.

It was from the supermarket's customer services department. While I didn't use my bank or credit cards while shopping en-femme, I had used the loyalty card which was registered to our home address and they'd found my details in the database.

The letter was polite and sympathetic – hoping I'd recovered from the attack in their car park. It also said that they were arranging for a bouquet to be sent to me.

The problem was that it was addressed to Mrs Williamson. Could I bluff my way out of this?

"I didn't tell you about the attack because I didn't want you to worry about me."

"That's not the point. And, I think you know it."

"What do you mean?"

"It's addressed to Mrs Williamson. Now I thought that had been a silly mistake. But I phoned the store and spoke to the security person who helped you. She was convinced that she'd been dealing with a female. So, it's not the name on the letter that's wrong. So, tell me the truth. Were you dressed as a woman when you were attacked?"

I considered lying, but I was cornered.

"Yes, I was."

Her face screwed into a sneer.

"Why? Why were you dressed as a woman? And don't say it was for fancy dress."

I felt a combination of relief to have it out in the open – and fear at what might come next.

"I'm transgender. I know you believe that's a sin but I don't think it does anyone any harm."

"It's an abomination. It says so in the Bible. That's what Reverend Parker and I went to Manchester to protest about. That and gays. Now you tell me you're one of them. It's disgusting."

"Why? You're wearing trousers. Why is that OK but not for me to wear skirts? And when did trousers become male clothes and dresses and skirts female? And, if you believe that chapter of the Bible, why do you wear clothes made from mixed fibres? Isn't that also forbidden?"

"God made man and woman as different. It's wrong for one to pretend to be the other."

"But, if there is an omnipotent God who made us as we are, he made me like this. If he's a loving God surely he wouldn't do it to torture me, would he? I've tried time and again to stop dressing but the urge is inherent and part of me," I argued.

"He only puts temptations in your path that you can resist with his help," she insisted. "It's unnatural you don't get other animals having homosexual sex or changing sex."

"In fact, it's not unnatural. Other animals change sex and some that are half one and half another. And there are dozens of species which have homosexual relations."

"Rubbish," she answered. "In any case, it's irrelevant."

I thought about trying to continue the debate – but didn't see any point. Lucinda wouldn't be convinced.

"You're going to have to choose to stop your disgusting behaviour or lose Olivia and me. We're not going to live with a pervert and you needn't think you'll get access to Olivia if we divorce."

We slept in separate bedrooms that night. I tossed and turned fighting with the dilemma. I'd tried several times before to stop dressing but had started up again after months or, in some cases, years. It was often the smallest thing that started me off again.

Could I succeed this time?

If I didn't, I knew it would cost me Olivia. I suspected Lucinda was already lost and I didn't particularly care about that. Perhaps I could resist the urge long enough for Olivia to finish her schooling – after that, it wouldn't be as important for the family to stay together. I had previously stopped for nearly four years. If I could manage that again, maybe it would be enough.

"Well?" Lucinda asked when I joined her in the kitchen the next morning.

"I'll try to stop. I know it won't be easy but I'll try. Maybe I can see about some counselling."

"I'm sure Reverend Parker can suggest someone who can help – or you could attend one of the Church's prayer camps."

Chris' story continues in Book II of the Impact Series.

Book 2.   1999

Chapter 1.   New Start

I tried. Honestly, I tried.

I got rid of all of my female attire under Lucinda's supervision. She insisted that we drive up to Manchester that fateful weekend. She was horrified how many outfits I had and wanted to know how much it had all cost. She handled everything as though it was contaminated. Most of it went to charity shops. Not the more intimate items, obviously. They went in the bin.

She insisted that I grew a beard and moustache to make it impossible for me to go out dressed en femme and made me have a short haircut. She searched the flat in Manchester from top to bottom to ensure that I wasn't keeping anything. She even checked my bank account and credit card bills for a while to ensure I wasn't renting storage space somewhere.

It was a pointless exercise. If I'd wanted to hide any of my female items, I could have asked Liz to store them for me – or found a cupboard at work. But I genuinely tried to stop dressing so I wasn't hiding anything.

I even agreed to attend Bible classes at the Liverpool church that had accommodated the delegation from St Johns for the protest at Manchester's Mardis Gras parade. But.....

If you enjoyed 'Impact', I'd be very grateful if you could leave a review on Amazon and Goodreads. Thanks.

NB Cover Illustration for Book 2 is temporary 'placeholder' and subject to change.

About the Author

 Helen identifies as female with a transsexual history - her preferred pronouns are she/ her. She grew up as a RAF Brat and dreamed of being a pilot herself but failed the medical due to having had hay fever (the RAF considered it risky trying to land an aircraft and sneezing at the wrong moment).

Throughout her childhood and early career in PR, advertising and marketing and getting married and having a family, she concealed the secret that she was transgender.

In 1998, Helen accepted that she needed to transition. Losing one job as a consequence, Helen joined Greater Manchester Probation as IT help desk manager in 1999. As the first openly trans employee nationally she provided awareness training for probation and prison staff (and others) and became the de facto lead on trans issues.

Helen persuaded the then Lesbian and Gay staff association (LAGIP) to extend its membership criteria to include trans and bisexual members and spent several years as chair. She also helped to found a:gender - the UK pan-Civil Service trans support network and was made an honorary life member when she retired in 2015.

She served on local and national diversity boards and chaired a trans charity in Manchester as well as training as a counsellor. Her work was recognised with several awards including a Butler Trust Award presented by HRH Princess Anne at Buckingham Palace.

Since retiring, Helen has continued to present workshops on trans issues and provide counselling for trans individuals. She also became a volunteer with Diversity Role Models - going into schools and talking to students about homophobic, transphobic and biphobic bullying.

Overall, Helen estimates that she's met well over 1,000 trans individuals who would previously been described as transsexual and many more who do not plan to transition permanently including cross-dressers, gender fluid, non-binary, drag artists/drag queens and some who identify as she-male. The discussions she's had with all of these individuals mean she has a huge wealth of information to draw on for her stories to ensure that they are authentic.

Helen started writing short stories for Cross Talk, Northern Concord Trans Support Group magazine, in the mid/ late 1990s — and started to write a novel while she was 'between contracts'. That novel was put on hold when she started working for Greater Manchester Probation in 1999.

After surgery in 2000, she joined Spice, a social activity group, in Manchester and did a number of adventurous events with them. This led to her colleagues asking, on Monday mornings, what she'd done at the weekend.

Typical answers were driving a tank, flying a jet, sailing a yacht, riding a quad bike or a hovercraft. Her colleagues told her that she'd led such an interesting life, she should write her autobiography — so she did.

While recollecting memories for it, she recalled an incident when she was 19 and living in London, described below under Summer Dreams.

Since retiring, Helen has been a member of the Manchester Women's Writers' Group which has provided valuable feedback on her work. Her story is covered in her autobiography: "A Tale of Two Lives: A Funny Thing Happened on the Way to the Palace".

If you enjoyed *Impact*, follow Helen on Facebook at:

https://www.facebook.com/helencaleauthor/

or her website http://www.helendaleauthor.info

Also By Helen Dale

Helen's books are available through leading outlets on line and (to order) in the high street.

Fiction

Summer Dreams

"Summer Dreams" is an authentic story of the transgender community and illustrates the wide range of trans people's experiences, the problems, prejudices and fears that they face (and some of their own prejudices) – and the fact that being trans is just one facet of their lives. It was inspired by a true incident when the author was about 19.

But let Vicky tell you about Summer Dreams:

I was David, but now I'm Vicky.

I was sunbathing in sand dunes near Bournemouth in 2003 when Roger found me and changed my life. After spending a heavenly holiday with him as Vicky, I just couldn't face reverting to David. I knew, though, that becoming Vicky permanently was impossible.

There was only one option, I tried to kill myself.

Roger saved me then showed how life as Vicky was possible.

Summer Dreams tells of my transition journey, coming out to family and friends and their reactions, some of which were very difficult to deal with, especially Peter my twin brother's and the abuse we faced from him and others.

But being trans is just part of who I am. Roger and I have a normal life too.

But is it too good to last?

What other readers have said:

"Brilliant"

"LGBT meets Howard's Way*"

"A page turner"

"Informs about trans issues without pushing it down the readers throat"

"It's a really good introduction to transgender issues and a romantic novel very well written"

"It's proper steamy"

"John didn't put it down beginning of lockdown, kept saying his glasses were steaming up"

"I really liked how Vicky was kind, caring and non-judgmental. Even though she's lucky, she still offers her help to Mia. Even though things seem to go smoothly, the book still shows the after thoughts and insecurities."

"An interesting viewpoint in the life of someone transgendered, the difficulties faced in life, and also in transition, many of which I had not considered. The basic storyline is sound, though I did find it a little 'wordy' in places, especially with the smaller details in regards to sailing, flying, and of routes to various places which seemed unnecessary to the story. Having lived in and around Southampton for 45 years I did enjoy, and imagined precisely, descriptions of pubs and places and I have been to. A good effort though for a first novel."

"Romance … and some sailing! This short novel follows Vicky as she falls in love with a man who seems too good to be true. But Vicky faces obstacles that you don't often read about in romance. She's a trans *woman and we follow her through surgery, through the process of coming out to her family, via various yachting incidents, right through to... well you'll have to read it to find out."*

"Great characters, a compelling story and a healthy dose of realism. Helen Dale tells it like it is and you can't help cheering for Vicky in all her trials, hoping that she gets to live 'happily ever after'."

ISBN Paperback   978-1-9996329-3-9

Inspiration for Summer Dreams

In 1966, while living in a bed-sit in SW London, I caught a train to Bournemouth.

It was an old styled corridor train and I changed in the toilets; putting on an orange bikini under my skirt and top. I took the Sandbanks ferry across to the beaches and dunes at Studland where I swam then sunbathed. As I lay there, I noticed a guy watching me so I quickly dressed and left.

But what if I hadn't noticed him?

What if he'd approached me?

What if he hadn't minded that I was trans?

Maybe, then, Summer Dreams wouldn't have been a work of fiction.

Changes

A tale of corruption, blackmail, revenge, drug smuggling, murder, and self-discovery told from five points of view:

Nigel Hall has a comfortable life running his advertising agency and using girls and other activities including sailing and trips to casinos to entertain his clients.

George Collins enjoys perks that Nigel gives him and doesn't worry too much about the invoices he approves.

John Ives hadn't expected to take his cousin **Carol Ives**'s part as Cinderella in a panto when she injured her ankle horse-riding nor that photos from the event would later give his fiancée an idea for getting him in and out of her parents' house without their knowledge. Nor did he expect to discover how much he enjoyed cross-dressing or that his fiancée would support him.

Then **Mary Sanchez**, the widow of OJ, a former business partner of Nigel, returns from the USA. She takes over the company George works for and extracts revenge on Nigel, who she blames for OJ's death.

The consequences impact on all of them.

ISBN

Paperback   978-1-9996329-6-0

What other readers have said:

'A gripping page-turner

'Helen Dale has written a sexy, exciting novel as seen through the eyes of five well-rounded main characters. I especially liked John Ives who had to ask himself some very searching questions when he discovered he enjoyed dressing as a woman - although this did come in handy on more than one occasion.

"Changes' is a thrilling page-turner with a heart-pumping finale. I read a huge chunk of it during a long plane flight and I couldn't wait for the return journey so I could immerse myself in it again.

Operation Busted Flush

Faced with attacks on their community by the White House Administration, a group of transgender veterans decide to take action

'"And I say the time for waiting is over. He's tried to stop us serving in the military. He's tried to withdraw rights we've fought for. He wants to prevent us using appropriate washrooms. Now he wants to eliminate us completely – they've even taken down every reference to transgender off government websites for Christ's sake! Enough is enough. We have to f*****g do something!" Angela slapped her hand on the table.'

ISBN Paperback   978-1-9996329-5-3

What readers say:

"I thoroughly enjoyed this novella. It follows the antics of the President of the USA 2016 to 2020 and his aggressive attitude towards the LGBT community. A group of transgender ex-soldiers vow to take their revenge.

I loved the scenes in the cabin where they were plotting with military precision how enact their plan. I was with them all the way. There were also moments of tenderness – planning for a wedding and support for the grieving. I have very little experience of the trans community but now realise how hard they have fought for their rights in society and what a massive impact the attitudes of national leaders have on their everyday lives. A real page turner - I couldn't wait to hear what happened next and it kept you guessing to the very last page."

"Transgender avengers form a crack team to take down a corrupt and authoritarian US president before he causes more harm to their community. Good action-adventure romp with wish fulfilment for all those who have watched in despair over the past years as our hard won trans rights are attacked by governments worldwide. Thoroughly enjoyed it."

What readers say:

"Some great short stories about the dilemmas of being a TV in the early 80s 90s. The diaries reveal a hidden community proudly remembered for its peer support, mentoring and deep friendship. full of spirit and life."

ISBN Paperback   **978-1-9996329-1-5**

Non-Fiction

A Tale of Two Lives

(A Funny thing happened on the way to the Palace)

Inspirational story of award-winning trans activist,

writer, trainer and counsellor: Helen Dale.

Having grown up as a RAF Brat and keen scout, dreaming of being a pilot in the RAF, she concealed a secret for decades before accepting, in 1998, that she needed to transition.

Losing one job as a consequence, Helen joined Greater Manchester Probation in 1999. As the first openly trans employee nationally she provided awareness training for probation and prison staff and others and became the de facto lead on trans issues.

She persuaded LAGIP, the then Lesbian and Gay staff association, to extend its membership criteria to include trans and spent several years as chair. She also helped to found a:gender - the UK pan-Civil Service trans support network and was made an honorary life member when she retired in 2015. Helen served on local and national diversity boards and chaired a trans charity in Manchester as well as training as a counsellor.

Her work was recognised with several awards including a Butler Trust Award presented by HRH Princess Anne at Buckingham Palace.

"A Tale of Two Lives" tells how she came out to family and friends and how that might have been handled better! It also covers her life after transition, embarking on a range of activities learning to scuba dive, qualifying as a yacht skipper, fire breathing, diving with sharks - including Great Whites - and holidaying around the world as part of a group or on solo trips showing that being trans is no barrier to living a full life.

Now available with colour Illustrations

ISBN

Paperback: (b/w illustrations):   978-1-9996329-7-7

Hardcover (colour illustrations):   978-1-9996329-9-1

What people have already said:

"an excellent read and filled in some of the gaps in your eventful life. It was a brave thing to write it but I would not expect anything less from you"

"I've read the book and found it very interesting, down to earth, no holds barred, and for me personally extremely helpful in understanding a close relative in a similar situation. Well done, I look forward to the next one."

"I loved this book and as my son is experiencing some of the same issues it gave me insight. I also bought the book for him which I think helped, though he has chosen not to transition. He chose instead to tell his closest friends and felt able to do that."

"A book about journeys and self-discovery and how to weather life's ups and downs. Fascinating insights into Helen's transition story richly peppered with the fullness of family, friendship, work and really living life to the full. Yes, Helen you have made a difference."

"I really enjoyed this book which covers the very interesting life story of Helen.

It's a really good read and keeps you interested as well as explaining more about the TV/TS community and the struggles they can face. Highly recommended"

"I loved this book and as my son is experiencing some of the same issues it gave me insight. I also bought the book for him which I think helped, though he has chosen not to transition. He chose instead to tell his closest friends and felt able to do that."

Understanding Gender Variance -

A Practical Guide: including Intersex, Trans, Non-Binary & Gender Fluid Individuals

Helen Dale has been involved in the trans community for more than twenty years; initially providing support on the internet then training as a counsellor and counselling supervisor; chairing trans and LGB&T support groups and providing workshops on trans issues to a range of audiences – and has won several awards for this work.

This guide has been developed from those workshops and her personal experiences supporting other trans individuals.

It is intended to be easy to read keeping jargon to a minimum and explaining terms in simple language. The information is laid out in logical sections – with a comprehensive contents section to find relevant details easily.

With the number of individuals identifying as trans, intersex, non-binary or gender fluid doubling about every five years, if you haven't previously met or had dealings with a trans individual, you may well do before long whether as a manager or support worker friend or family. It will help you to identify the questions that you need to ask and how to avoid common mistakes. It will also be a valuable resource for anyone who identifies as transgender, intersex, non-binary or gender fluid.

The book is aimed at anyone dealing with trans people:

- Counsellors / Help-line Operators/ Befrienders
- Support/ Social Workers
- Union Staff
- Teachers and Lecturers
- Citizens Advice Bureaux
- Samaritans
- Criminal Justice System staff including
- Equality and Diversity Practitioners
- HR staff
- Other Managers
- LGBT+ organisations
- Family & Friends
- And Trans Individuals themselves

Contents include:

- Definitions
- Causality
- Social Transition
- Transsexual Journey to Surgery
- Travelling on: Post Transition / Surgery
- Trans Issues in Counselling
- Partners and Families
- Case Studies
- Legal History
- Discrimination & Hate Crime/ Incidents
- Employment
- Trans People in the Criminal Justice System
- Bibliography

Hard cover version includes colour illustrations; paperback version illustrations are black and white.

ISBN

Paperback (B/w illustrations):   978-1-9996329-3-9

Hardcover (colour illustrations):   978-1-9996329-8-4

What readers have said:

"Your books were the first thing I found that made sense from a human point of view instead of science and big words."

www.ingramcontent.com/pod-product-compliance
Lightning Source LLC
Chambersburg PA
CBHW072010210726
48294CB00013B/1833